Playing the Game

Dorothy W. Cosey

ISBN-978-1-105-21866-8

DEDICATION

I dedicate this book to my younger brother Lavern for his help with the character Al Freight and for opening my eyes to some of life's harsh realities.

CONTENTS

Acknowledgments i

ACKNOWLEDGMENTS

To all the young men in our country that believe the way to be successful is through the mighty dollar. My hope for you is to read this book and find the courage to leave the game and to value the greatest treasure in the world LIFE.

To my three nephews Johnnie, Daniel, and Devon thank you for your love, support and being my models for the cover.

To my younger brother Lavern, I got nothing but love for you little brother. Thank you for helping me with the character Al Freight and teaching me about life on the streets.

Prologue

Toney Harris was born in 1962 the one son of Margaret and Bill Harris. The family moved to Chicago Illinois when Toney was sixteen years of age his mother a homemaker and his father worked in the manufacturing industry for over twenty years. To look at his family it seemed normal to the untrained eye, but to those who lived in the neighborhood knew otherwise.

Bill Harris was a womanizer. One of his favorite past times drinking and chasing every single woman in sight. When things went wrong with one of his many women in the street, Margaret Harris would feel the brunt of his vicious temper.

Toney remembers several nights that Bill Harris came home late from work, and started augments with his mother. Some arguments were so violent that Toney would wake from a sound sleep.

There was more than one occasion that Toney has to intervene, dragging his dad off his mother, when he was beating her down as a man. Toney tried several times to get his mother to leave, but she refused. She was hoping that her husband would eventually change which never happen. The fights continued in his household sometimes Toney was on the receiving end.

He made the decision to leave home living in the street and befriends two other boys going through the same thing. Al Freights family was immigrants from Italy. T-bone and his little brother Stacy came to Chicago from the south.

The boy's friendship developed into a bond, and soon they became crew, gang banging in the streets. Their hustle was selling drugs, committing crime and petty theft. Toney became so absorbed with the game and his crew school takes a back seat for street life. Toney, T-bone, and Al Freight were notorious thugs. The three men had women quick cash and were reckless.

Toney survived in the streets two years after leaving home. At nineteen, he was cocky and arrogant. He met a girl named Joann Watson kicked it with her for a short time. Then she showed up on his doorstep pregnant with his son Marcus. Toney came from a violent family and he was not about to let his child go through the same.

He married Joann gave his son his last name. Joann pleads with Toney to get out of the game, but her advice falls on deft ears. He was a thug, a rough neck, and has the respect of his boys. No woman was about to dictate his moves. He continues diving deeper into gang life and crime for three more years without incident. Joann was pregnant again with Yvonne and the money was running out.

Toney has to make a decision. Instead of leaving the game and finding legitimate work, he settles for a quick dollar involving a drug dealer. Actually, the plan was introduce by his two homeboys Al Freight and T-bone.

The plan was to rob the dealer of his drugs and then sell them in the street to line their pockets. Everything was plan to the wire, until Al reneges on the deal. The men rolled up at the dealer's house, and break in. They search for the drugs, but find they are not alone. The dealer spots them in his home and draws a weapon. Al shoots the man killing him instantly. Toney froze not believing the robbery could go so wrong. Al Yells over at Toney "Let's move man" and dashes out the door. Toney was about to make a move to leave when the cops showed up.

The dealer had a security system installed in his home. Al Freight runs to the vehicle without Toney. T-bone was the wheelman. He asks Freight in a distressed voice. "Where is Toney?" Freight replies, "I told him to let's roll. We have to leave now." Travis (T-bone), was not about to leave his friend and argues with Freight. "I am not going to roll out without our boy man."

Al puts the gun to Travis head forcing him to drive off. Toney stands in handcuffs charged with murder and robbery. Bill and Margaret Harris attend his sentencing along with Joann and their son Marcus. Toney stands in an orange jumpsuit shackled with chains on his feet, and handcuffs on his wrist. He waits for the judgment to come down.

The Judge looks at his extensive criminal record and sentences Toney to fourteen-year's hard time. Margaret Harris drops to her knees with both hands in prayer. His father bows his head wishing he had done a better job raising Toney to be a decent man. Joann hugs Marcus. He was two years old as tears stream down her face. The sight of his family grieving rips him apart. Looking at his mother and Joann was almost too much to bear. The guard leads him from the courtroom.

Chapter 1

The strong winds push against skyscrapers, blowing loose debris into the streets, trails of paper swirl in the air barely missing the pedestrians walking along the busy sidewalks.

The forecast for today cloudy with a chance of snow, Marcus Harris watches from his high rise building people scurrying along. It was never quite in Chicago that was for damn sure a brother needs a little quite time, just to get their thoughts together.

He takes a deep breath before going over last night in his mind. Remembering the scene at the club with his boys Trigger and Durango, they were drinking chilling at the club when all hell breaks loose.

The three men hooked up at one of the cities hot spots. They roll up on the scene, styling their name brand gear. It was obvious to anyone familiar with the fast lane these brothers were balling, and sporting gear that cost a fortune.

No one could cop their swag, most brothers spitting hater aid, but that was nothing in the hood. You get use to envy, that never changed. After paying the cover charge, the three men walk into the door, security pats them down.

No guns or weapons allowed. They move deeper into the building. The music is loud, and the club crowded beyond capacity. You could hear people trying to converse over the music.

One of Marcus friends calls over to them. He has a booth and asks them to join. It was Stacy one of his mother's former boyfriends.

Stacy was a smalltime pimp he would not let go of the game even though it cost him his freedom more times, than he was willing to count. It was the norm for him. They make their way over to Stacy. "What up dog? What you doing in here?"

Marcus also known as Marco answers the question, "Just out hanging man

trying to see what we can get into tonight."
The man nods his head in
acknowledgement. "Who this?" he was
looking in the direction of Trigger and
Durango.

Marco makes the introductions.
"This is my crew Trigger, and Durango.
Chill Stacy their cool. What is up with the
booth Stacy? You are doing it big these days
huh?"

The man smiles flashing his gold
tooth before answering the question, "You
know how we do man. How's your momma
with her fine self?" "She's good man, still
doing her thing keeping me on the straight
and narrow."

Stacy looks at Marco with a grin,
"It's all good, wish I had a momma like
yours when I was your age. Maybe I would
not be in the game right now. I would have
stayed in school instead of these streets."

Stacy orders another round of drinks
before asking his next question. "You are
still in college right? Stick with it man, do
not let these little fast tale girls get your nose

open out here." Marco leans in the seat to put emphasize on his words.

"I got you man, you know what it is, business before pleasure. Right now all I'm trying to do is stack my paper, I am thinking about going to California with my old man, He tells me there is a lot of opportunity for a young brother."

The man thinks on Marco words. "I hear you young brother. Keep your head up, and grab any opportunity to do better man, that's real talk." Durango spots a girl, and wants to kick it with her. He has been trying to hit that for the longest.

He gives us the signal before leaving the table chasing after the female that caught his attention. "Look here brothers. I will get at you in a minute, going to holler at that Shorty over there. See you in a few." We give him the high five he was always trying to add another female to the list.

My boy Trigger is passing the blunt. "Hey man this place is full of fine women tonight." He was eyeing a big booty girl standing by the bar. "Hey Marco man I'm gone dog, need to handle some business, I hear baby calling my name.

I'll get at you in a few." I do our little hand shake before he jets from the table. He was on his way to holler at that girl. Stacy and me pass the blunt we talk some more. Our conversation ends, when a brown skinned honey steps up to our table. She was eyeing me. Looking, me up and down with that come-hither look in her eye.

"You want to dance" she places her hands on her wide hips. Judging from the expression on her face, tells me she is accustom to having her way with men. "Hold on one minute Ma." I pass the blunt back to Stacy, and wink at him. Stacey knows I am on the prowl. He gives me the high sign, as I move from the booth.

It was my turn to check her out. She was a dime you could not deny that. She has an oval face, smooth skin, and full lips. She is wearing a designer brand outfit.

The short skirt compliments thick thighs, and well-rounded bottom. Her waist is small, and full round breast get my full attention, baby is stacked. She was the type of chick that brothers fight to keep. I cannot deny she looks good. Nevertheless, was it worth all the problems that come along with a high maintenance babe like her?

Guess I am going to have to find out. I answer her question. "Yeah Ma let's do this." She succeeds, and satisfaction accompanies her smile. She shakes her hips walking towards me, and reaches for my hand. Together we walk to the dance floor.

I pull her close on the dance floor getting ready to put down some serious game on her ass. I mention I am in school working on an Engineer's degree.

I make it clear that I work! I am not one of the usual broke brothers hustling in these streets. She is listening. I do not mention my sideline job that is on the down low.

My boy Trigger is across from me laughing. He knows I plan to hit this tonight. We make eye contact, each knowing where this is going to lead. The woman I am dancing with interrupts my thoughts.

"You seem different. Most brothers are looking for a woman to take care of their ass. You seem to have life figured out." I smile down at the Shorty, "Yeah Ma, you know my momma raised me right. A man handles his business."

I ask some more questions the important ones because I am not looking for any drama right now. "You got a man Ma?" She raises her head from my shoulder, looks directly at me then answers.

"Are you applying for the position?" I respond the way real players do. Handle this like a business transaction. I already got more women than I can handle. I hesitate for only one moment before I answer her question.

"Is the position available?" It is my turn to watch her sweat. She pauses for one second then replies. "Yeah baby that is why I asked."

I look over at my boy Trigger still watching this go down. I nod my head, and wink at him. He already knows where I am spending the night. I turn back to the honey waiting on my reply.

"Cool then I accept the job, when can I start?" She leans closer into me, pushing her body against mine, and in a seductive voice replies. "Right now, why don't we call it a night and you come over to my place?"

I put baby on hold only for a second. "Let me holler at my boys for a minutes, order a drink, and chill Ma."

Just when I release this honey to go over to my boys, a big dude is charging towards the dance floor. The man walks over toward Trigger who is slow grinding with the big booty chick.

The Dude grabs Trigger by the shoulder. They are face to face, and he demands to know what Trigger is doing with the big booty chick? She was his woman.

I alert my boy Durango, we both move toward the big dude who is checking Trigger. My fist close cause I already know trying to talk is going to be out of the question.

The big dude's crew is approaching fast, and they surround my boy Trigger. He looks around to see if we are on the way. Once he catches sight of me, and Durango pushing through the crowd, he stands his ground.

Do not get me wrong, Trigger is no punk. He would shoot your ass in the blink of an eye. It was Triggers turn to check the big dude. "Hey Man, you better slow your roll. You need to be checking your girl. I was told she has no man."

The big dude was not trying to hear any excuses. The big dude shoves my boy Trigger, and his crew is instigating the situation. One man yells. "Beat that fool down Corey."

Durango and I get past the onlookers. We are standing in the circle next to our boy Trigger. At this point, Trigger and the man named Corey square up. They are ready to do battle. My fists are still closed, and my stance is defense mode.

Trigger moves fast as lightning. He bows his head, and tackles Corey. The two men hit the hard floor exchanging blows.

One crewmember attempts to kick my boy Trigger. I let loose on his ass, striking him with so much force blood spews from his mouth. Durango is going at it with another one of Corey's friends.

The fight is even three on three. Right now, I am so angry. I am kicking ass and taking names. After about thirty minutes into the fight Corey's friends decide they have had enough, they back up.

Durango and I pull Trigger off Corey. The man is unconscious. Trigger is struggling with us not wanting to let this go. He yells out. "Let me go man! This sucker wants some of me. I will give his ass what he asked for."

I hold on to Trigger. My boy has snapped. "Come on man let him go. You have whipped his ass. Let's bounce man, before five-O gets here."

Trigger calms down. We do our handshake. He does the same with

Durango, and he leaves the club. Durango and I do our handshake. As I make my way over to the honey that, I plan to go home with. The girl checks me for injuries after she is satisfied we leave. I am driving at a high rate of speed.

The girl next to me mentions that her name is Brenda. It dawns on me. I did not care enough to ask what her name was. Brenda is making idle chitchat. You would think she was nervous or something.

I notice the difference between us. She was nervous, but not me. Going home with a chick was nothing. I have gone home with so many different honeys in my twenty-three years. I lost count.

Only one thing was on my mind, hit it, and quit it. Brenda is giving me directions to her home. I slide in, and out of the lanes heading to the south side down 112th street.

We pull up in front of an apartment complex. It was a huge gray building surrounded with iron fence in the front. The building has some type of security. She waits for me to open the car door.

I go over to the other side, and pull the handle. She steps out, and puts her arm around my waist. She was putting on a front for her neighbors. I guess Brenda does not want them to get the wrong impression. This trips me out. It did not take imagination for me. What I was after with this chick was sex. Then I am ghost.

We enter the elevator. Brenda leans into me once more. She pulls my head down against her mouth. She was teasing my lower lip, nibbling on it, and tracing her tongue around my mouth. I could hear her moans, soft barely audible. She continues to tease my mouth with her tongue.

Her hands are in my hair pulling at the thick mass of curls. She is standing on tiptoes. I have to lean down to kiss her, since I am over six feet tall compared to her five-foot stature. Baby was doing her thing, and I was enjoying the foreplay.

The elevator dings before the door opens, and Brenda pulls herself together. I am cool just a little firm. She holds my hand, and we walk to her apartment door seventeen G.

She unlocks the door, and asks me to make myself at home. Brenda wants to change into something more comfortable. I look around the room the place was spotless. At least she was a good housekeeper. I stroll across the room to look at a couple of photo's sitting on a table. One photo was of her parents. The rest I assume are friends, or family.

Then I make my way over to the portable bar, and have a drink. The alcohol disappears in one quick swallow, and I pour another Hennessey and coke. Then I feel hands on my body. I slowly turn and Brenda is standing there in some lingerie. Her body was banging in the skimpy outfit, and my manhood stands in attention after embracing her loveliness.

She leans into me again closing the distance were our bodies became one. I bend my head down to kiss her lips my tongue finds hers and play together for a few minutes.

She was draining me of my strength my hands cup her backside pulling her closer to me, my mouth finds the softness of her neck. I kiss it slowly moving downward.

My hands move over her well-formed body caressing her shoulders, and down to her waist. She begins talking incoherently still pressing herself against me. My mouth is next to her breast I pull back the material and lower my mouth to her nipples.

She shivers from my touch I continue holding her flesh against my mouth sucking slowly on each one moving my mouth up and down letting my tongue make tiny circles.

My teeth nibble on the tips of her nipples, they become erect from the motion, and baby is moaning my name she wants it, but I plan to make her ass beg for it.

I continue my assault on her senses, grinding my manhood against the softness of her. She feels me, her hands search wanting to touch and feel all of me.

She is kissing my nipples drawing them to her lips. I feel the roughness of her tongue, but it excites me more than I have imagined. She is taking off my shirt, and her hands still searching touching, I feel her hands on my buckle she unfastens the obstacle between us.

My pants fall from me. She is pushing my underwear down past my knees. My manhood erect and throbbing for all to see, she looks at it, holding it in her hands then moving up and down in a single motion she is caressing me holding on feeling the blood rush into my organ.

The next thing I feel is her mouth on me. Her mouth is warm , there is a vacuum effect from her bobbing her head up and down chanting to herself as she continues to masturbate while holding on to me in the other hand.

I begin pumping my hips in rhythm. She continues circling her tongue in every direction. I let out a moan "Oh Baby just like that." Until I could take it no longer, I finish undressing her.

She is naked standing before me. I lift her in my arms, and go into her bedroom. After I place her on the bed, I join her, rolling my body on top of her. I play with her then lift her legs and enter that warmth.

With quick thrust hitting her from all sides then I break it down to a slow roll she is moving with me holding on breathing as if it is her last breath.

Our sweat mingles, I turn her over then pull her against my manhood from behind she is going crazy talking out of her mind I continue with quick thrust until we both collapse from the exertion. After it was over, I roll off her onto my back looking at the ceiling.

She snuggles against me asking the question no player wants to hear. "Will you call me? Can we go out again? I really would like to see you again." There was a pause, she is waiting for my reply, I have too many honeys already she would have to take a number but for now, I would tell her what she wants to hear. "Yeah baby, I'll call you alright."

I roll off the bed go to the bathroom and take a quick shower, I can see Brenda is disappointed. She thought I would spend the night, but there is no need to make her think this was a relationship, cause that is not what it is.

I look at myself in the mirror what stares back at me is a brown skinned male with thick curly hair arched eyebrows and a goatee mustache. Yes, brother has it going on.

I know I look good, too many women tell me the same thing. They all want a relationship, but I am an educated rough neck, still in the game making my money, stacking my paper. Women in my opinion are for my pleasure, one day I will settle down, but not today.

I finish my shower drying off my body, and Brenda is standing in the doorway. "You really are going to leave? Let me love you all night long baby." I smile at the woman sure, I would put it on her ass again if I had the time, but right now, I need to catch up with my boys business before pleasure.

"Yeah baby that's all good. I would love to do you again, but I have some business to take care of I will call you."

Brenda presses the issue, "I really want you to stay here with me can't you do whatever later?" My patience is running thin I need to be on the move. "Look baby I said I will call you, peace." I move past her, picking up my gear after I was dressed I walk out the door without a backwards glance.

The elevator was open I rush in when I finally make it to the ground level. I jump in my ride and head out back to the south side of town calling on my cell Trigger answers, "Hey man you and Durango ready to do this?" "Yeah man scoop us up we are ready."

I head over in the direction of seventy first street south side pick my boys up then over to one hundred Seventh Street to do business with the Freight family. Yeah this was my other profession selling stolen inventory off boxcars.

The pay was good and we were in and out in a matter of minutes. In Chicago, everyone has a hustle this was one of mine. We have our assignment for tonight. We start in the direction of the assigned rail station.

Once we reach the location, I kill the lights and sit in darkness as the runners throw off freight. I start up the engine then ride alongside the train collecting the inventory loading it in my truck.

Time to roll we head into the assigned location making the drop at a neighborhood garage, our contact pays us on the spot. He informs us they have another assignment later in the week, and would keep in touch.

We leave the vicinity I drop my boys off and I head for home. It is four in the morning I grab a couple of hours of rest I have class in the morning. My alarm is going off. I throw back the covers and get a quick shower.

I check my appearance making sure my gear is tight, then out the door to

Chicago University. After class, I stop over one of my girl's house, and smoke a blunt with her.

Gina and I have kicked it for a long time. She knows I am unfaithful, but she continues to hang on. "Marco, when are you going to be ready to settle down? We have kicked it for two years baby. I need a commitment." Here she was always trying that same old ploy, which never works. "Why baby? We work fine as we are. I give you good sex when you need it and no strings baby more of friends with benefits."

She rolls her eyes, once again frustrated with my ass. "Marco I want more than a body next to me when it's convenient." I get off the couch holding the blunt. She was blowing my high with this crap.

I put out the blunt and try to smooth things over. "Look Gina baby we are good leave well enough alone baby." Gina is a good girl we been getting down since she was sixteen we started dating for a couple of years now.

I am standing behind her, wrapping my arms around her, kissing on her neck, trying to change this subject because I know this is not what I want right now.

I want to build my career then I can think about a family. She gives in to the seduction, turning around to face me as I hold her in my embrace. She puts her lips against mine we kiss. I go hard on her demanding her surrender.

It was so easy for me to get a woman under control all I had to do was tell them what they want to hear the rest was easy.

I watch Gina go through all sorts of emotions. She wants to tell me no, but not having the strength too. My seduction continues my tongue slides in her ear nibbling her neck my hands palm her bottom.

My mouth covers hers deepening the kiss our tongues mingle with one another, my hands move into her panties. My fingers massage her until she begs me to give her release. That sound was music to my ears. I had her where I wanted her under control.

We make our way to the bedroom she is begging me to lay pipe, but I am not ready yet. I manage to get her out of the rest of her clothes then I continue with my seduction. "Oh Marcus, baby give it to me baby." How many women have asked me for the same thing? I lost count, but right now it was Gina my main girl begging so I had to put it on her ass.

Chapter 2

I put my hands on her hips drawing her closer to me on the bed. She squirms withering in ecstasy as my hands work her like a bad habit. I continue dipping my fingers into her wetness.

She calls my name repeatedly talking in gibberish. I place myself inside her warm moister she pushes her backside against me I push harder until I fill her up. She continues to beg for more and I give her what she asks for.

We reach our climax together I shudder from the release. She rolls over to look at me. "Marcus, I love you boo." I am breathing hard right now, I just put in work and she wants to have a conversation. "Yeah baby I love you too." I was on my way to sleep.

After a couple of hours, my cell rings, it was my Mother Joann. "Marcus

Terrell Harris, why have I not heard from you lately?" I think of a quick excuse. "Hey momma, I was going to drop by today. I have been busy with school."

My mom pauses for a couple of minutes. "I am glad to hear this son, but I would like to see you today. What time are you coming by the house?"

I look at my watch my shift starts in a few hours at the Bank. "I am on my way now. See you in twenty minutes, love you mom." Gina is ready to protest. "Marco, I thought we could spend the day together."

I roll off the bed grabbing my jewelry, and my gear. "I have to take a rain check on that Ma, I'll holler." I hurry, putting on my shoes. It was time to exit stage left. I kiss Gina on the cheek then walk out the door. As I make my way to the car, I remember I need to change my vehicle.

You never use the same car long it made it harder for five-O to identify your ride. In the freight business, it was just a smart move.

I start my ride heading to the nearest car rental in the area, and walk up to the front desk. A young woman greets me. I complete the paper work with one of my fake ID's, and she gives me the keys to a new Dodge pickup.

I continue in the direction of South Lake Park where my mother resides. It has been a couple of months since I have been back in the neighborhood nothing changed same old players hanging on the same old blocks.

I continue walking towards my mother's building, and enter the elevator. I ride it to the ninth floor.

My mom checks the peephole then opens the door. "Well my son never thought I would have to beg for a visit." She was smiling at me. I lean over and give my Momma a hug. We walk inside her apartment before I make any conversation.

"Are you alright Mom? Is everything good?" My Mother is five feet five slender build, brown skinned with a pretty face. She worked hard taking care of my sister Yvonne and me. After working her way through school she lands a job as a Bank manager, right now life was good.

Joann waves her son over to the couch before answering. "Everything is good son, your sister is doing well with her family and you know I stay busy. The question Marcus is how have you been?"

I did not like lying to my Mother. She was proud of her son. I never been arrested was not involved in any gang banging. I was a good student in school, and used my job working on computer systems for the bank as a front.

I had all my bases covered. I played the game the prodigal son and brother living different lives. I am a rough neck in the streets committing crime, a college student on honor roll. I played more women than I care to count. How long could I keep it all straight? I answer her question. "Yeah Ma I'm good, just focusing on school and working you know the usual." My mom is watching me, she knows me to well at least she thinks so.

"Marcus you sound like some damn advertisement son. We want to see more of you." I stand to hug my Momma, I try to make excuses but if it means that much to her I will show up more often.

"You will see more of me promise, I got to get out of here. Need to go to work, I love you Mom." Joann stands on tiptoes and kisses her son on the cheek. "I love you too Marcus."

My breathing slows down when I exit my Mom's apartment. One of my fears is dying in these streets or getting caught-up riding dirty.

That would kill my Mom that was the last thing I want. I push that thought from my mind. My phone is blowing up, and I ignore the call. Just some random females wanting me to sex their ass, but me I am all business.

I jump in my ride heading down 87th street toward my job. I check my attire the suit looks good, I have a clean cut appearance going on right now.

Yes, I fooled many people with my image no one was the wiser about my activities except my boys and they were down for me for life.

The bank is in view. I pull into a parking space, and kill my engine. Then take a second look at myself through the window of my car.

After I was satisfied with my look, I stroll into the bank. Everyone greets me. I ask to speak with the manager about my work assignments. I go into the office and Carol West asks me to take a seat.

"Morning Marcus, you need to see me? Have a seat make yourself comfortable." She walks over to her desk and sits down in the chair. I clear my throat.

"Yes Carol I need you to reschedule me next week I have a couple of things I need to take care of , would it be possible to switch my days?"

She looks at me for a couple of seconds before replying. "Umm, let me see Marcus, you are an excellent worker and I don't have any trouble out of you let me go over the schedule, and see if I can shift a couple of things.

Now understand I cannot promise you that I can make this happen, but I will try. I have your number. I will give you a call this evening. Is there anything else?"

A smile plays over my lips, I know Carol will make this happen. There is no doubt about that, she dropped her panties when I first started working at the bank.

Marcus remembers Carol is a freak in the bed and she always calls him when she wants good sex. Sure, she would make this happen, because she likes the way he puts it down in the bedroom.

"Okay Carol thanks I appreciate it." He stands looking directly in her face, and pauses for one second. "Like you said, you got my number call me." She caught his meaning.

Carol admits Marcus is her boy toy she would defiantly give him a call this evening. Marcus leaves Carol's office with a smile on his face reminiscing about whom was playing who?

She thinks she has him under control, but in reality, he was playing her. Marcus ran game on women all the time. Carol was not the exception each session with Carol lined his pockets. Carol pays for the private sessions, one thing for sure he was no one's free ride.

A sly grin was on his face, it was just too damn easy to make a woman do what he wanted them to do. He strolls down the hall entering empty offices with computers in need of repair. He puts his phone on vibrate and continues fixing the broken computers.

His pants leg is vibrating off the chain probably one of his girls on the line, it would have to wait until later. It was seven o'clock time to get up out of here. He checks his phone for the missed calls earlier. It was his boy's number.

What the hell, they both know his work hours he dials Trigger first. "What's up man? Dude why you calling me at the job? You know I am trying to stack my paper."

Trigger sounds strange like he is stressing over something. "Look man, meet me at, the diner on thirty First Street, we need to talk man it is real important." This was not his boy Trigger at all he sounds worried as if something has him shook.

Marcus thinks over the question there was no way he would leave his boy hanging no matter what the situation. He answers Trigger. "Yeah man you know I am there.

What is the deal Trigger?" There was a pause, "I can't talk on the phone man we can do this in person I will see you in thirty alright." Marcus replies "Alright, peace Trigger."

He shoves the phone deep into his pocket Marcus was concern. His mind goes over every detail of the conversation. What could have his boy sounding scared?

He has known Trigger all of his life, he could not remember a time when Trigger let anything worry or stop him when trouble came knocking. What happen to change all of that?

Marcus packs up his tools and rushes out the door. He unlocks the car and pushes the speed limit trying to catch up with Trigger. He was making good time another block and he was at the diner a little hood restaurant named Memories.

He looks around taking in his surroundings this was gang territory. He opens his glove box and retrieves the nine, just for insurance that he leaves in one piece.

After he puts the gun into his waistband, he pulls on a hoodie shirt, and exits the vehicle. Hookers and junkies begging for a dollar greet him.

Marcus keeps walking trying to avoid a confrontation with anyone his main concern was to see his boy then bounce.

He enters the restaurant the waiter rushes to take his order. He orders an iced tea then searches his surroundings looking for his boys.

Trigger and Durango wave him over to a table in the corner. He sits down with his boys. He is looking at the expression on his crew's face it causes him concern.

Marco hesitates for one moment then asks the main question. "What is all this secrecy shit man? You two acting like five-O is looking for you."

Trigger answers first. "Look Marco we have a little problem. You know that chump Corey from the club. Well it seems that homeboy has a couple of connects in the city. These punks threaten my Moms the other day.

Corey sent some random thugs to rough her up a bit man. They told her they were sending a little message from Corey.

Marco takes a deep breath before replying. "Is your Mom okay man?" Trigger is clearly irritated from the episode. "Yeah man she is a little bruised and shook from this shit."

Durango responds. "We need to holler at Corey man. I mean strong let this punk know what the business is man.

Marco interjects. "How strong you want to come at this dude man? I do not think this fool will take threats lightly. We are going to have to eliminate this problem for good, you feel me on that?" Trigger thinks on Marco's suggestion.

"Well, you brothers know I have no problem putting his ass down, but we have got to have each other back. We got to make this happen without one of us taking the fall."

Marco digests this information. Was he ready to kill for his friends? Was he capable of taking another man's life if it comes down to it? He goes over every avenue, there has to be another solution to this problem?

Maybe a good beat down would put some fear in this fool better that then the alternative. He mentions this option to his friends. "Let's keep that on the back burner only if there is no other way. I think we need to have a little talk with Mr. Corey first then if this fool wants to take it further we will come at him hard."

Trigger is irritated, and voices his distress. "Come on Marco don't bitch up on me man. I know I am asking for a lot but I need to eliminate this problem. You know I would do this for you man."

Marco's temper spikes from the comment. "Chill Trigger, you know there is no bitch in me! Do not go there with me man. You know I am down for your ass. We are crew but you have to use your headman, we are talking retaliation and prison if this shit goes wrong.

We will holler at him first if that will not stop this shit then I am down with whatever." The two men think on Marco's words he was right as usual, they all have a lot to lose.

Trigger admits Marco is his right hand man. Marco would not desert him when he needed him the most.

He offers his hand to Marco. "I'm sorry man you are right we have to think. You know I prefer to settle some shit, and worry about the consequences later." Marco accepts Triggers hand they do their handshake.

"It's all good Trigger, I got you man. I would feel the same if this went down with my family." Durango teases his boys. "You two quit. You make me think there is love in the game." They all laugh.

Marco's cell phone begins to ring he looks at the caller ID thinking it was one of his honeys. Instead, it was Al Freight, it must be important because Mr. Freight only calls his runners if there was a problem.

Marco signals his boys to chill and takes the call. "What up Mr. Freight." "Marco, glad I caught you. I need you and your crew this evening. I got an important shipment coming in tonight can you make it?"

Marcus hesitates for one moment before answering. "Yeah, that's cool we can be there what time?" "Better make it at two-thirty in the morning this is a special shipment, and I don't trust anyone else with it."

Marcus becomes suspicious. AL Freight continues his conversation. "Marco you and your crew know loyalty is important in this business that is the only reason I have selected you. Keep that in mind while working for me."

The line goes dead. Marco gets the impression that there was a threat in Al Freights message. He wonders why Mr. Freight thought it was necessary to remind him.

Durango and Trigger notice the strange look on Marco's face something was wrong. "Hey what is up with the phone call? I have never heard of anyone talking with AL Freight."

"That makes two of us because I have been hustling with the Freights for two years and never once talked to the man." Durango asks. "What's the deal Marco? What does he want? What happen to our connect that set up all the runs for us?" The three men look among themselves that was the question of the evening.

Trigger looks a little worried. "Man something is foul here we all have been getting onboard with the Freights and we always used his connect. What the hell is going on here man?"

Durango replies. "Dam man I hope this is not some FED shit because neither one of us need that shit." Trigger responds. "I' am with you man this shit could be some kind of set up man." Marcus answers. "Calm down brothers, we make too much money for the Freights.

I doubt this is a setup but there is defiantly something wrong with this picture. Look be ready I will scoop you up and we will roll together then maybe we can get the answer to our questions."

Marco's phone was ringing again this time it was Carol from his job. A smile touches his lips, yeah he knows what this call is about and he would give her what she was looking for.

He answers the call once again signaling his boys to chill. "What up Carol?" The woman on the other end was breathless like she was working out. "Hey Marcus, I am at the gym right now, but want to know if we can hook up around nine does that work for you?"

Marcus winks at his boys, laughing silently. He knew he would receive this call eventually. "Yeah, Carol that sounds good. I will see you at nine." Carol continues. "Marcus, bring your big gun. I want to play tonight are you up to it baby?"

Marcus smiles once more. It was funny that she always asked for it but when it goes down, she could not handle it. She was too busy screaming her head off.

He answers her question. "Yeah right like you could handle it." There was a pause. "Just bring it baby when you come, we will see who can handle what."

He ends the call. Durango was the first to respond. "Well Marco, judging from the look on your face you about to run up in some female, so when are we going to handle that Corey situation?" Marco was not off point he was always business before pleasure. "I say let's locate this brother put the word on the street see what we catch.

Then my brothers we handle Corey agreed." Trigger did not like this shit but he rolls with it for now.

They need more information on Corey where he hangs out and with whom. Trigger would even go as far as hurting someone Corey loves. He was not playing games when it comes to his family, especially his Mother.

The men agree Trigger and Durango would put the word on the street it should take a day at the most then they would handle Corey. Marcus leaves the restaurant. He checks his watch it was close to nine now. He jumps in his ride and heads out towards Carol's place. Her address is in South Lake Park Area. He pulls into the driveway her car is out front, and he knocks on the door.

After a couple of minutes, she opens the door wearing a skimpy outfit. Marcus realizes she wants to role-play again. Cool he was with it. Before he could close the door, she was all over him.

You could smell the alcohol on her breath she was building up courage to release her inhibitions with the drink in her system. She starts talking dirty. "Did you bring my big gun? You know how much I like to play with it."

Her hands slide down my pants groping me like some kind of sex maniac, she is backing he ass up against my manhood, sliding up and down trying to get me in the mood.

I ask in an understanding voice. "Carol, are you drunk? Look Ma we do not have to go there if you don't want to." She turns to face me. Her face is full of excitement she purrs.

"This is what I like Marcus now call me a whore talk dirty to me baby you remember how I like it." I did what she asks it was her fantasy. "You whore get on your knees and kiss my feet."

She does what I say this was crazy as hell, but I continued calling her obscene names, and the more names that I call her the more excited she becomes.

Carol is defiantly a freak. The insults excite her, and she pulls me towards the bedroom. Once we make it to the bedroom, I notice that the mattress has several adult toys lying on top of the mattress. Carol picks up a wooden paddle and hands it to me then asks.

"Will you beat my ass while we are having sex? And Marcus keep talking dirty I love it."

Chapter 3

I accommodate her. When she was finish having her way with me, I mentioned my paper for all the sexual acts.

She replies. "No problem baby it was worth every dime, I will call you when I need you again." I catch the hint and glad to leave this dysfunctional broad she needs a lot of work. I collect my paper take a quick shower dress and out the door.

I call on my cell Durango answers. "What up dog?" I reply. "Hey man lets hit the club tonight we got a few hours to kill." "Okay man I'll hit Trigger up which one tonight?"

It takes me only one moment to reply. "Let's hit Deuces tonight, see you in twenty." "Bet." I roll up to the spot pick up my boys then head to the club. When we arrive I change my hoodie for my suit coat, my gear is still tight.

We pay the cover charge, and enter the building females are against the wall talking with the men, and we head towards the bar.

We order a couple of drinks and find a seat in this crowed club. Trigger and Durango are not on the hunt for females tonight.

We are all business each in our own thoughts concerning the shipment we are about to deliver. A couple of females approach the bar, asking us to buy them a drink. One of the women is heavyset, and her front teeth have gaps. The other female looks like a skinny crack head.

We called women like this chicken heads and they were defiantly that. My boy Trigger rudely dismisses the women telling them to get out of our face. After they refused to take his advice, he starts tripping. "Look you bust downs get the fuck gone bitches." The heavyset woman begins cursing at Trigger. He loses patience with the woman, and makes a move to rise from his seat.

I place my hand on his wrist to restrain him; we did not need this right now. Then I apologize to the women, and offer to buy them a drink to calm the situation down. It works they accept the drinks then leave.

I turn to face my boy Trigger. The look on my face says it all, and I come at him hard. "What is up Trigger? You ready to knock around a female now. What is the deal man?"

For one brief moment, Trigger looks embarrassed, but that soon changes to indignation. "What the fuck Marco, you trying to chastise me now? Over some bust down hoes, are you fucking kidding me?"

Durango can see there is about to be an altercation between friends, and attempts to intervene. "Chill you two we are boys. It's not that serious, relax." We are still staring each other down. Trigger is not going to budge and neither am I. I slice the silence. "You keep testing me Trigger! I am not one of these punks you bully in the street."

This time Trigger does something that surprises us both. He gets off the seat, and stands to face me. I never thought this would happen. We were friends since elementary and today we are adversaries.

I follow his lead and stand to do battle if necessary. Durango once again tries to squash the argument. "Hold on man. I know we are not going there, what happen to us being crew? This shit is not worth it man. You two chill."

Trigger looks at me as if I am a complete stranger. Then he replies. "Marco, you had better know who you are fucking with." I am astound this could not be my boy, the one who has my back on everything. Now this motherfucker is threatening me that was not going to fly.

My temper gets the better of me I shove Trigger and he retaliates. Durango is in the middle trying to make us release one another. He manages to separate us but we are ready to cross a line that we have never crossed.

Durango lets out an execrated sound. "Dam man what is up with you two, come on man we have enough to worry about without you two being at each other's throats. Just chill brothers, let this go."

I relax for one second, try to calm down, and figure what is going on with my boy Trigger. I exhale my breath then apologize to my boy. "Look man, you can talk to me. What in the hell is going on with you man?" Trigger looks like his world is coming apart.

His face shows frustration and worry he suddenly hugs me and apologize for his actions. I return the hug. Trigger was one of my best friends we grew up together, laughed, and cried together since we were knee-high.

I realize he is upset about the episode with his mother, but it was something more going on with Trigger and I was determine to find out what has my boy acting crazy.

I look around the club searching for an empty table when I find what I was looking for I ask my boys to join me so we can talk. They follow. I start the conversation. "Okay Trigger what is going on man and keep it real no bullshit be straight up with me." It was hard for a man, a rough neck to confess his sins.

I could see from the look on my friends face he was having a hard time. He looks at Durango, then me, and bows his head and replies." I fucked up man, I did some shit that can have all of us in deep shit."

Durango and I are staring at each other both wondering what Trigger is talking about it was not long before he begins to confess. "There are a couple of things I did not tell you. The incident with Corey and my Mother was retaliation." Durango and I look at each other again.

Trigger continues. "After the incident in the club, I caught up with Corey. I paid a couple of dope feins to rob him of his stash. He knew I set the shit up, I was going to teach his ass a lesson, but it backfired.

You know my mom's has a drug problem well she found his drugs. You already know where they went, well that left me high and dry we are talking a lot of money here." I interrupt him for one second. "Exactly how much doe are we talking Trigger?"

Trigger looks over at Durango and me; he takes a deep breath then replies. "Over thirty thousand man, I could not believe she would go through that much smack, but she did and now I have this shit hanging over my head, but that's not all man." I was silently holding my breath. Durango's eyes were about to pop out of his head we both are in disbelief.

Trigger continues. "I was desperate! I went through my cash with the clothes and the honeys. I could not replace Corey's drugs and I did not have the money so I hooked up a scheme to get the money.

I stole some merchandise from the Freights that is why you received the call. Man, I swear. I was sure no one saw me rob the warehouse; I waited for all the runners to leave that night and murdered our contact. Then I took the merchandise." Trigger put his face in his hands breaking down in racking sobs.

Durango and I fall back in our chairs both shocked by Triggers revelation. Time stands still, and I could hear my heart pounding in my chest. A thin film of perspiration forms on my top lip. I run my hands through my hair stunned not expecting this type of behavior from my boy.

Then I start to think, and what crosses my mind makes me ill to my stomach. Was Trigger so low down that he would let Durango and myself walk into the line of fire?

Was he even going to tell us before we went on this run? I tried to make myself believe that this was my boy for life that he was not capable of this type of deception.

Another part of me knew he was capable of this type of shit, and that hurt more than anything did. I try to calm myself down because anger is silently sleeping inside of me. What Trigger did can cost me my life, freedom, and career? Those were small problems in comparison.

Trigger and his actions will force me to stay in the game and that is not where I want to be.

I am so pissed off right now I cannot speak. Durango breaks the silence. "Man do you realize what you have done? I understand you wanted revenge but you beat this dude down in the club that should have been enough.

You have jeopardized all of us. We no longer have the option of dropping the game because you have put us in the mix with the Freights." Trigger lifts his head he looks like someone beat him up. He waits a couple of seconds before he replies.

"Man I know. Where do you think this leaves me? I did not think man I did the shit without thinking it through. If it was just me I could handle the consequence, but this is my Mother, and I put her in harm's way."

He lowers his eyes then looks directly at me. "Marco man, I know you are angry and I respect that man, but we are crew and I need my boy's with me right now."

He was waiting for my response. I sit up straight in my chair because this was unbelievable. It was like some sort of nightmare that I could not escape. All I could see was my future going down the drain. Here I am in more danger than I know and the one thing that is on my mind is my Mother.

This shit will kill her if she ever finds out. My whole life was unraveling right before my eyes and there was not a damn thing I could do about it.

My mind is racing when I look at Trigger, and my expression displays frustration. How could he be so stupid? "Look dog, this is way over our heads this could get all of us killed. Man we are crew, I am down with you."

Trigger was silently holding his breath. He releases it then asks Durango the same question. Dupree (Durango) was sitting back in his chair with a concerned look on his face he was aware that they really have no other options. "I am down with you also Trigger."

The men would ride this out to the end with their boy even though it could cost their lives and freedom. Trigger asks the next question. "Are you ready? It's time to see Al Freight."

We slowly leave the table, each wondering how this meeting would go. I do not know about my crew, but as for me, in the back of my mind I already knew something terrible was about to take place.

We roll up at the rail station sitting in darkness waiting for the signal. No one says a word because we all are facing the unknown. I spot the runners they are using the bolt cutters on the doors we pull up next to the train and the freight is loaded into the back of my truck.

My nerves are on edge, I have done this one thousand times but today fear was driving, I have never been this afraid. It was like having a realization of what all this could mean if something goes wrong.

We load the last of the freight a sixty-inch television, and then into the night we are ghost. My heart is pumping a mile a minute until I see the garage in view. Once we park, we exit the vehicle and speak with the contact.

This time it was different, we enter the office the man waiting is not familiar to either of us. He introduces himself as Taft. One thing for sure he was wide as any linebacker, and the aura about Taft borders on thug mentality.

Trigger asks the question that is on our minds. "What up Taft, when do we get our bread?" The man is observing the three of us then waves us to a take a seat. "Hold up one minute fellas, Mr. Freight would like to thank you boys personally."

You could smell the fear in Trigger. His eyes were bulged, and a thin film of perspiration covers his forehead.

Durango looks over at me he was feeling the same vibe as myself. We were not fool enough to think this was a social call, no something was about to take place.

I could feel it in my gut. Someone was going to pay the price for Triggers foolishness.

We did not have to wait long. Al Freight arrives but he was not alone. This was the first time I have met the man. He is large in stature, his hair is sprinkle with gray and he looks like one of the mobsters you read about or watch on television.

The other men enter the room with AL Freight. One is a teenager about eighteen at the most. The young man looks afraid for his life. An uneasy feeling washes over me something is about to go down.

The man named Taft gets to his feet he shakes hands with another big man named Max. "Hello Mr. Freight." Al Freight nods his head in the young man's direction. "Take care of our little issue Taft."

Taft walks over, and picks up the gray masking tape off the desk. He turns in the direction of the youngster. The man named Max shoves the boy down into the chair. Max is holding the young man down while Taft binds his wrist.

Once they complete the task, Max begins to wrap the tape around the teenager's chest. The boy was trying to struggle as if he knows what is about to happen.

Taft continues wrapping the tape around the boy's feet, confining him to the chair. The youngster eyes are wide with fear. Al Freight directs his attention to my crew, as if we are an afterthought.

"Which one of you is Marco?" I take a nervous breath, and then slowly rise out of my seat. Al Freight was around two hundred-thirty pounds at the least. I look him directly into the eyes, what stares back at me are narrow silver slits filled with anger.

I square my wide shoulders and stand to my full height. "That would be me Mr. Freight." The man looks me from head to toe. He walks closer to me, before I realize what is happening his hands are around my throat.

His face was only inches away from mine. "Today I will teach you and your crew the price for disloyalty." Trigger and

Durango are on their feet, I glance at my boys who are ready to take these dudes down.

I give them the signal to stand down there was no way we could handle the three of them. AL Freight acknowledges the eye contact and releases the pressure of his hands on my throat. He narrows his eyes looking directly at my crew.

"You aren't as dumb as you look, first lesson don't cross a mob boss it could prove fatal." He releases his hold, and pushes me toward my crew.

My boys check to see if I am okay. Al Freight walks over to the desk and leans against it not taking his eyes off either of us. He rubs his hand against his five o'clock shadow before he replies.

"Well Marco we have a little problem, one of my contacts was murdered the other night, and I am missing a lot of inventory. How long have you worked for my organization?"

I think over the question and almost laugh aloud. How could he not know how long I have been down with his organization?

My better judgment tells me to answer the question. "I have been down with you over two years."

Al Freight shifts his gaze on Trigger and Durango. "And what about you two, how long have you worked for me?" The men answer the question they all have been down with the Freights over two years.

Taft and Max are standing hitting their fist into the palms of their hand. They are waiting for the signal to eliminate the three of us. I could hear my heart beating like a drum.

For the first time in my twenty-three years, I felt like my life was going to come to a terrible end. It was a waiting game the man is staring us down waiting to see if one of us would crack.

Trigger is sweating bullets. Marco and Durango would not sell him out to Al Freight he was willing to bet his life on it. The problem was guilt was eating away at his conscience. None of them would be in this predicament if not for his stupid pride.

After about fifteen minutes of a stare down, Trigger is ready to take the fall, but before he can confess his role in the robbery. Al Freight does something that surprises us all.

He walks away from my crew and me and continues his questioning of the younger man. "Alfonzo you have a history of shortages with inventory. This leaves me with one person responsible for the robbery and murder of my contact."

The boy named Alfonzo is out of his mind with fear. He vehemently shakes his head in denial. "Mr. Freight, please I swear to you I never stole anything from you. I never killed anyone. I put this on my life."

Al was not trying to hear anything from the man named Alfonzo. He nods his head in Taft and Max direction. "Marco, you three hold on." Al orders my crew and me to sit tight.

The two men approach Alfonzo, Max has a pair of bolt cutters in his hand,

and Taft has what looks to be a switchblade. Max places a large piece of tape on the boy's mouth to silence his screams.

The man named Max takes Alfonzo's hand in his, and snipes one finger off with the bolt cutters. The man screams in agony. Blood covers the floor. Al Freight watches without showing any emotion.

He turns his gaze back to my crew and me waiting to see if we would make a move. He shoves his large hands into his pockets and replies. "You want to make a profit off of me this is what happens.

No one steals from me and gets away with it." He nods his head again, and Max continues torturing the young man. You could hear Alfonzo's screams and they went on for over twenty minutes.

I watched in horror as Max cut off every one of Alfonzo's fingers until the man passes out. The floor covered with Alfonzo's blood, and his screams echoes in my ears. A wave of nausea overtakes me.

I am holding my head in my hands sick from the sound and sight of death right before my eyes. When I manage to keep the nausea down, I look up thinking this shit was over to my surprise they continue mutilating the young man.

Taft takes his knife slits Alfonzo's throat then reaches inside the incision, pulling his tongue through the opening. The boy was dead. Taft directs his comment to my crew. "This is a mob neck tie, remember that."

Al Freight instructs Taft and Max to get rid of the body. The men cut the tape that was holding Alfonzo then drag his lifeless body from the room. You could see a trail of blood and his fingers on the floor.

Al walks over to the desk opens a drawer, and removes a few vanilla folders, after looking at the information a couple of minutes he replies.

"Marcus Terrell Harris AKA (Marco), Dupree Johnson AKA (Durango), and Tyrone Davis AKA (Trigger). You see I know everyone that works for me. I also know your parents, and siblings."

Chapter 4

Al pauses for the revelation to sink in. "Now let me tell you three how this is going to go down. I' am in need of your services on the regular. You will be at my disposal, no questions asked. What you witnessed here today stays here. Do we understand each other?"

We nod in agreement thankful that it was not one of us tortured by Max and Taft. Al tosses the files on the desk. He was staring at me with those lifeless eyes. "Marcus my advice to you is to count your blessings.

The only reason I spared your life today was not for you, but your father. Ask him about me, he will tell you, I am not a merciful man."

It was over. We could leave, as we walk out the door the smell of human flesh burning was in the air. I dare not look in the direction the smell was coming from.

I already know it is Alfonzo's body burning beyond recognition. I quicken my steps wanting to get as far away from Al Freight and his organization as possible.

I believe I was at a run making my way to my vehicle. My crew was right on my heels we all are afraid. Once we are inside my ride we talk.

Durango was first to start the conversation. "Did you see that shit? Man we are in serious trouble, what are we going to do?" Trigger was shaking inside, but he manages not to let us see it.

"Man, that young dude lost his life because of me. I have to live with that dog."

Once Trigger mentions Alfonzo. Vivid images appear in my mind's eye. I could still hear his agonizing screams. It replays repeatedly in slow motion in my mind.

I will never forget this day as long as I live. My hands are shaking, as I grip the steering wheel. I take a couple of deep breaths trying to calm myself down.

This was the first time I have to admit I want to shed tears, but I am a rough neck, and a man that was not an option.

I take another steading breath before replying to Durango. "There is only one thing we can do man and that is what Al Freight says, if we value our lives."

Durango responds. "Man we have lost control of our lives. We are in deep, and this was not my plan for the future, as far as I can see, man we are stuck."

Trigger answers. "Look dog, I got us into this mess and brothers I plan on getting us out, one way or another. I owe you that much. None, of you would be in this mess if not for me."

After Trigger finishes a flash of anger overtakes me. This fool has caused me to become a full time criminal. His stupidity has changed my whole life, and still he is talking about a get back.

I could not hold my peace. "Hold on dog that is the last thing you should be thinking about. There is no way in hell we can take down Al Freight. For now on you let Durango and me do the planning agreed."

Trigger was pissed, and has a problem with Marco ordering him around, as if he could not come up with a successful plan. This irritates him, but he realizes he is helpless without his crew backing him.

Trigger regains his composure before he answers. "Cool Marco we will do this your way." At least I got him to agree to that much. I have to get control of Trigger he was tripping and his recklessness could cause our lives.

I start the engine we roll out pushing the speed limit to the max wanting to be as far as possible from the Freights. I let my boys know that we will hook up tomorrow.

"Hey brothers lets meet tomorrow we need to figure how to straighten this out with Freight. We are going to have to get him off our ass. That is real talk."

At least we all can agree on that. I am at the point that I do not care how or what I have to do as long as it gets us all out safely.

I drop my boys off and head toward home. My mind is still going over the turn of events. I decide it was time to give my old man a call. Freight told me to ask my father about him.

Maybe my dad could shed some light on this situation. I check the time on my watch it was four in the morning. I decide to wait until after my class then I would put in the call to my father.

When I make it home, I crash for a few hours before class. The alarm is going off I rush and shower and change my gear out the door for class.

I sit in my class trying to focus on what my professor is demonstrating. Some random females are trying to holler at me on the low.

I smile at them, but a female is the last thing on my mind at this moment. After class was over, I jump in my ride and my phone starts blowing up it was my boy Durango.

"What up dog?" "Hey man I got some info on our boy Corey. You still want to handle that man?" I think for a quick second then reply. "Yeah man, where is our boy Trigger?"

"I haven't heard from him as of yet. I got that word this morning, and called you first. I will call him where you want to meet at?" Give me a few minutes man lets meet over at Memories in twenty."

"Bet, see you in twenty, peace." I hang up the phone start my engine and roll in the direction of Memories restaurant.

After, I make my destination I walk into the restaurant and my boys are waiting on me. I take my time stroll over to them and we talk a few.

I start the conversation. "Alright brothers how you want to handle this fool? Trigger answers before Durango. "You know what my suggestion was from the get man.

Let me peel his cap, and we will not have to worry about a get back man." I hear Trigger talking but his answer for everything is violence. At this point killing matters to me.

I was no killer. "Hold on man. You are tripping again man. We agreed to beat him down if necessary. Smoking, this dude was last options remember."

Trigger cuts his eyes over at Durango then me. "You know Marco man you are acting like a punk right now. What is the matter man? Al Freight got you shook?"

Before I know it, my temper snaps with Trigger. "First off Trigger you should be the last brother questioning my manhood. You are the fool that got us in all this shit in the first place.

If you think punk is in me, then you try me, and find out." Trigger sits back in his seat. He is watching me as if he was wrestling with himself not sure, how this would go down.

Then he smiles at me looking sheepish. "It's all good man we are boys. You know I just be playing with you Marco." Durango replies. "That is the problem with you Trigger.

Everything is a joke to your ass. I am not feeling this man. I have a career, and woman to keep safe. We are in deep with the Freights because of you, and in the mix with Corey because of you. Maybe you had better chill Trigger before you find yourself assed out."

This was the first time Durango was questioning their association. He sounds like he is at his end with Trigger and his antics. I sit back watching my crew and question the same things.

If Trigger does not slow his roll there may be no future for all of us. This is defiantly not, where I want to be that is for sure.

I try to calm the situation down with my boys, and get back on point. We need to handle Corey that is the first task on our agenda. "Chill you two. We need to find this fool Corey and handle business."

Everyone agrees on that subject. We leave the restaurant, and head in the direction of fifty Third Street to a local bar.

It is early in the day, and brothers are standing outside of the business.

We park then exit the vehicle. A couple of brothers outside are familiar we greet them then continue inside the establishment. The building is dark it take us a minute for our vision to adjust.

We scan our surrounding and then notice Corey with a couple of his boys at the pool table. The plan was to get Corey to leave the building with us at gunpoint but once again, Trigger deviates from the original plan.

Before we know what this fool is planning, he walks up to Corey. "What's up now fool." Trigger pulls his pistol on Corey. The man is ready to deal with whatever, showing no fear of the gun in his face. His boys wait to see what is about to happen.

This pisses Trigger off more. He strikes Corey in the face with the butt of the gun. Corey falls to the ground ready to do battle with Trigger.

He slowly rises to his knees, as he turns to face Trigger he feels cold steel against the side of his head. "What up now dude, looks like your ass is in a sling partner." I can hear the patrons in the bar scream. People are scattering in every direction.

Once again, Trigger has put us in a messed up position. I draw my heater so does Durango we have our guns on Corey's boys because we know they are packing. I disarm one of the men and so does Durango.

Our beef is with Corey not these cats. If Trigger would have stuck with the plan we could be out by now with Corey in tow, but instead we have to handle his boys. The only thing on my mind was no witnesses.

I have to see this to the end thanks to my boy Trigger. Today I became a killer. We usher the men out the door into my ride. Trigger sits in the back with these brothers keeping them at gunpoint.

Durango and I sit up front. I am driving away from the bar. Only a couple cats saw us leave with these dudes, and none

of them would go to the cops with that
information.

As far as anyone knows, we had a
disagreement between friends. We continue
into the rough part of town I park in front of
an abandon building we exit the vehicle.

Corey looks at his surroundings and
knows what is about to take place. He
responds. "You fools planning to x me out?
You have better have a backup plan
homeboy. My peeps will not let this shit ride
trust."

Trigger was about to hit Corey again
I stop him. "You're not in a position to be
running your smart ass mouth man. I think
you better chill."

The three men were not about to go
out like punks. Corey does a move and
knocks the gun from Trigger's hand. During
the chaos, his boys try to make a move but
my boy Durango was not playing games,
and opens fire on one man. The man hits
the ground like a ton of bricks.

Trigger was losing the scuffle with
Corey, while I am wrestling with the other

homeboy. The next thing I know my gun goes off. I shot this dude on accident. He drops like a leaf from a tree.

I was in shock. I killed a man, something I swore I would never do. When I turn to see, what the outcome is with Trigger I hear gunshots. Trigger shoots Corey at close range.

It was over no more looking back. I kept telling myself we are crew and it was for the good of all concerned.

We leave the scene shook from what has taken place in the abandon building. I glance at my watch it was noontime. In a short period of two hours, I committed a murder, and none of this was part of the plan.

We roll to my crib change our gear placing the bloody clothing into a garbage bag. Durango volunteers to dispose of the evidence.

I wipe off my heater place it in the bag my crew does the same? No one talks for a couple of seconds then the reality of what went down comes crashing down.

My heart is racing so fast I feel nauseas. I let the emotion pass then direct my comment to my boy Trigger. "Man what is the deal with you? Are you some kind of magnet for trouble? What happen to the plan dog?"

Trigger straightens up his position from a slump to standing in agitation. His brow creased in anger. "Look Marco, what the fuck did you want me to do man, wait for this fool to smoke all of our asses?

I interrupt his tirade. "What I want you to do man is follow the plan not deviate when it is convenient for your selfish ass." Trigger was incredulous. He could not believe Marco was calling him out once again. "So now I am selfish? Really Marco, I just saved your sorry ass life punk."

I was past caring what happens next. I was tired of Trigger and his recklessness. This time, I was determined to draw the line somewhere.

I was yelling at the top of my lungs. "No homeboy what you did is fuck up my future and my life. You want a thank you Trigger well hold your breath."

Durango steps back this time he would not be the mediator in this situation. He was over Trigger and his wild ass ways. We both stand facing each other. It was time to cross that line.

Trigger and I are staring each other down, both tired of skirting around the inevitable. I am ready for the altercation to start, and my phone begins to ring.

I glance at the number for one brief second. It was Al Freight. All the fight goes out of Trigger once again reminded that he needs the alliance of his boys. He takes a seat. I answer the call.

"What up Mr. Freight?" Marco glad I caught you. I have an assignment for you and your crew. There is another shipment coming in tonight-on seventy eight-rail station.

You need to be there at three thirty in the morning, collect the merchandise as usual. Marco there is one item in this shipment that I want you to guard with your life.

It is black and white Maytag washer. Deliver it to me." I was about to ask where, but he continues. The address is one hundred twenty six and Dewey. You cannot miss it look for a neighborhood garage the building is blue in color."

I remember the information. "Okay Mr. Freight got it." Al Freight replies. "And Marcus, drop the formalities. We are business associates. The line goes dead. I stand there a couple of seconds before I explain the details to my crew. Durango asks first. "What is it this time Marco? Where is that heartless bastard sending us now?"

Trigger remains emotionless he was tough in the streets, but even he knows that the Freights are no joke. He remains quite not one sound.

I answer Durango. "We need to be at the station on seventy eighth. There is one item of interest to Al Freight. We need to deliver it to the garage on one hundred twenty sixth and Dewey."

Durango looks irritated with the information, and replies. "Look dog I don't know how much more of this I can take. We just watched an innocent man die right before our eyes.

Less than three hours ago, we committed the murder of three people what the hell man. Now we have this bastard hanging around our necks. What is next? Are we delivering drugs?" That last statement hits me like a bulldozer. I was thinking now that was it all the important deliveries for Freight.

This blows me away. I sit down on a stool by my counter. That has to be it. It made me even more determine to cut all ties with Trigger and the Freights.

Back in California Toney Harris is enjoying his success. The only regret is not having his wife Joann or, his children Marcus, and Yvonne at his side.

Toney made it out of the game but not without paying a price. He sits back in his chair going over the past.

He was nineteen when he hooked up with Joann, and was heading down the wrong path from the start. He grew up with an alcoholic father, and a faithful mother. He remembers watching his mother go through hell with his dad. He spends each night wondering when she would finally get tired of his abuse.

He remembers her bruises, and the beatings they both received by his hand. Toney was not going to let this happen to any child of his.

To rebel against his father Toney let his grades drop in school. He spends his time hanging out with the thugs of the neighborhood.

Toney's crewmembers were Al Freight, and his boy Travis AKA T-bone. His neighborhood was a mixture of different cultures. It was easy to run with the wrong crowd.

At the time, Toney was dating Joann, a short time into the relationship; Toney gets her pregnant with Marcus. He did the right thing by Joann and married her except she would have been better off without him in her life.

He was not ready to let go of the game. The only thing that was important at the time was being with his boys, his partners for life. A cynical smile touches his lips.

What a fool he was to believe in partners for life. That was a bitter joke, and he was gullible enough at the time to trust his boys for life. Toney was on the loose chasing women and gang banging with his crew.

Chapter 5

He was notorious in the streets. Until a robbery goes wrong, and that is when his life takes a sudden turn.

He got away with crime for three years straight. Joann was pregnant again. This left him hard pressed to care for his family.

Al Freight and T-bone mention they are about to commit armed robbery of a drug dealer. Toney was down with his boys.

The problem was it did not go according to plan Al Freight murdered the dealer, and makes a quick escape. T-bone was waiting in the getaway car, and Toney was not as lucky. He did not exit the scene in time.

The police arrive and his crew dips out on him. Toney was holding the bag for the murder and robbery. The cops offer him everything under the sun to snitch.

Toney was no snitch. He was loyal to the crew and maintained his silence. He takes the rap for the murder and robbery, and sentence to fourteen years hard time.

Sure Al came to visit so did T-bone. The problem was he lost his family. Al would put large amounts of cash on his books. He also set up a bank account for Toney.

Al was grateful for Toney's silence. Years later Al goes on to become one of Chicago's biggest mobsters. Toney severs all ties with the game and his crew.

He moves to California after his release from the joint, but not before trying to repair his relationship with Joann. At thirty-six years, old Toney was starting over. He manages to get his degree in prison.

He was college educated in the joint. Instead of it being a disadvantage, Toney uses street smarts and invest the money Al Freight put aside. He starts a computer business, and it turns out to be successful.

Toney invests everything into the business. It takes six years, but it was well worth every dime. At forty-two years, old Toney was a business owner respected in his community.

His mind returns from the past. He checks his appointment book. Marcus graduation is in a couple of months. He would have to give him a call this evening. Toney scrolls his phone log and dials Joann.

The phone was ringing after three rings Joann picks up. "Hey Toney, how are you?" He waits for a couple of seconds. She still has a hold on his heart. "Hey Jo, I'm good. How are you? How are our children and grandchildren doing?"

Joann smiles to herself. Toney was on good terms through their divorce. She had no choice but to end their marriage. She exhales a breath.

How she wished things could have been different. "As far as I know Toney everyone is fine. You know, Marcus graduation is in a couple of months. I was debating on a graduation gift."

"Yeah, I was thinking the same thing. Maybe we can split the cost of the gift if that is cool with you."

Joann pauses for one second. She enjoys talking with him maybe she never stopped loving him. She answers his question. "Yes that would be great. You have any ideals for a gift?"

It was Toney's turn to pause. He admits hearing her voice was one of the highlights of his life. "Not at the moment Jo. Maybe we can discuss it over dinner. I am coming to town a week before graduation." She smiles again. He was asking her on a date. "That sounds good Toney. I would love to see you again. Umm, I mean to discuss our gift for Marcus."

He waits, she was accepting his invitation, and he dares to hope for something more. "Clear your calendar for the twenty-sixth of May I will be there, and Jo how is Yvonne, and the kids?"

Joann hears the concern in his voice. She answers. "They are fine. Yvonne is a good mother and wife. Her husband Dale treats her like a queen. She is very happily married."

Toney pauses again. "That is good to hear. My baby girl deserves the best. Jo, how are you really doing? You got yourself a new man in your life yet?" Joann was smiling ear to ear. "Right now I am single. What about you, any new women in your life?"

There was a short pause. Toney was smiling on the other end. "Not at the moment. I go on dates but nothing serious." He puts emphases on his next remark. "Jo, I am glad, you are single. My hope is to change all of that."

Joann feels comfort and contentment from Toney's admission. After a brief pause, she replies. "Toney, my hope is to let you change it."

His heart was beating fast listening to her words of endearment. He never stopped loving her. "Jo, I love you, talk to you soon." Her heart stops in mid beat for one moment. "Toney, I love you too, bye."

Toney sits at his desk reeling from the conversation with Joann. The admission of love for her shocks him, but it was out there now and he has no regrets.

He finishes work. The drive home is pleasant after talking with Joann everything was brighter in his life. Toney enters his home a spacious four bedroom contemporary condominium. He walks over to the bar and pours a gin and tonic. After a couple gulps, he tosses the jacket over a chair, and dials Marcus.

He waits for his son to answer. "Hello Dad, what's up?" Toney leans against his desk. "Hey son what's been up with you? You ready for graduation?" Silence greets Toney. "Marcus you hear the question? What's up with school son?"

Marcus was on the line trying to cover for his problems. He was torn. One part of him wants to share his life the other part fears losing his dads respect.

Marcus clears his throat before he replies. "Yeah Dad, it's all good. I am ready to get this over with soon as possible."

Toney laughs at the answer. "Is it that bad son? Judging from what your Mother has told me you are an honor roll student. No worries son." Marcus is debating about asking his dad about Al Freight. "Yeah you are right dad."

There is a short pause. "Um Dad, I need to ask you something." Toney was listing. "Go right ahead son. Just don't ask for something that will take me to the cleaners."

Marcus laughs. "Dad, it is nothing like that. I want to ask you about Al Freight. I met him a while ago, and he asked about you?

Toney almost drops the phone, how in the hell did Marcus come across Al Freight? Moreover, why was he asking about him? There was a long silence.

When Toney replies it was questions instead of answers. "Marcus, please tell me that you have not gotten involved with Al Freight."

Marcus remembers from visiting his father. He was patient and understanding man with a great sense of humor but right now, you could hear the anger in his tone. Toney replies. "Marcus, I am waiting on an answer."

Marcus was debating. What should his answer be? If he discusses his dealings with the Freights, it could cause him and his crew a lot of trouble.

What Marcus was trying to accomplish was a plan to get out of the game. He needs to know what he is facing. "Dad, relax. I am not involved with the Freights. I just met Mr. Freight on the street, he asks about you. Marcus lied.

Toney was not convinced Marcus was telling the truth. "Son, I am going to ask you one more time. How do you know Al Freight?" Marcus was playing a mind game like a chess tournament with his dad trying to predict his move.

"Man, Dad I just told you the truth. You do not believe your son now. Who is he Dad?" Toney takes a deep breath. One thing he never expects, is explaining his association with Al Freight to his son.

"Son, listen to me. I know you are not being truthful with me right now. If you are in some kind of trouble, please let me help you.

There is only one way you could know about Al Freight and we both know the answer. Marcus, stop trying to game me. I have played the game a lot longer than you."

Marcus panics. It was no way he would be able to convince his father. Toney was an old school player, and spent his young life in the streets, and that was something you never forget. Once you learn how to run game. You know game when you hear it.

"Dad, why do you refuse to answer my question?" Toney tries another approach. "I will answer your question if you answer mine."

Marcus subsides. "Alright, Dad I did a couple of runs for the Freights. That is how I know him." Toney was on the other end ready to explode. Marcus admission was one he dreads hearing. Why is he part of this type of mayhem? His mind is racing.

There is no logical reason for Marcus to be hustling in the street. He works, makes great money. He and Joann help with anything he needs. This was inexcusable behavior.

Toney takes a shaky breath. "Why in the hell would you be making runs for Al Freight Marcus? You cannot give me one good reason why you need to be hustling in the streets son." Marcus knows the lecture is coming he tries to avoid it.

"Dad, believe me I know this but that is hindsight right now. Marcus voice breaks over the phone. Toney hears the distress in Marcus reply. "Marcus what is it? How deep are you with Freight?

Marcus mans-up. There was no way he was going to get his family involve. That was the last thing he wants to do. Toney already did time in the joint. He would not let his dad lose his freedom again.

"Look, Dad I am good. You don't have to lose no sleep on that alright." Toney was not finished. "Marcus, anytime I hear my son sounding like something has him shook. I am concerned."

Marcus has to end this call, if waits any longer he just might confess his sins to his dad.

"Dad I got to go. I have homework and a date tonight. Do not worry I am good. I love you dad." Toney tries to stall him. "Wait, son if you need me for anything or you are in some type of trouble. You can count on me. I love you Marcus."

Marcus is holding his breath. "I love you too dad, talk to you later." The line goes dead. Toney knows Marcus is in some type of trouble, and it involves Al Freight.

He closes his phone and places it on the desk. He was trying to think of a way to come to his aid. Toney pours another drink, and walks back to his desk. He puts in a call to Stacy.

They go back a ways, and one thing about Stacy. He has the low down on what was going on in the neighborhood. Any smalltime pimp would have the four-one-one.

The phone rings a couple of times before Stacy answers. "Yeah, this is Stacy. What it is?" "What up Stacy? Long time no hear. This is Toney Harris, I need a favor man." Stacy acknowledges Toney. "What up Toney? You know I be looking out for your son man."

Toney appreciates that loyalty. "Good looking out Stacy. I need you to put your ears on man, let me know what is going on with my son. Today I discovered he is getting down with the Freights. You and I both know that is bad business."

Stacy is surprised. He thought Marco was smarter than that. "I got you Toney. Last time I saw Marco he was up in the club with his crew.

Man they tore the dam place up beating down a few fools in the club." Toney digest this information. "What crew is that some rough necks, or is he gang banging?"

Stacy responds. "Just a couple of college boys he runs with. I don't know much about them, but will do some research on them if you want me to man."

Toney thinks on the question. "Yeah man, give me the four-one-one on all his activities. I am more concern about Freight." Stacy tosses Toney some information.

"I got you man. You and I have history with Freight, that cat is bad news man. Word on the street is he smoked some young fool working for him a couple weeks ago."

Toney was well aware that Al was capable of murder. He witnesses it firsthand. "That is what I am worried about man. I don't want my son to become one of his statistics."

Stacy gets his meaning. Everyone knows Toney took the fall for Al Freight. "I got you Toney. We are old school players. Both of us have been in the mix with Al one time or another."

Toney relaxes a little. At least he has Stacy in his corner. They both share a common adversary Al Freight. "Thanks Stacy, I owe you man." Stacy acknowledges Toney's sincerity. "No problem man. I will get at you when I got some info. Peace Toney."

They end the call. Toney may have to make reservation early if Marcus is in as deep, as he believes.

Stacy leans back in his booth, and goes over the conversation with Toney in his mind. Toney was a good dude. Anyone that would take the rap for a crewmember's crime has his respect.

That was just the way it works on the street. You never give up your boys. Stacy makes the decision to have a word with Marcus.

He was going to pull his coat on a few things. Mainly his association with Freight, and then the real story behind his dads prison stint.

Maybe if he knows the real deal it will help him end his association with the

Freight family. One of Stacy's girls was approaching his table. The woman hands him her earning for the evening.

Yeah, he was an old school player, and so was Toney. His mind wanders to Joann. It would kill her to find out Marcus was in the game. One thing he was sure of Joann worked her butt off raising two kids while Toney was doing time.

Stacy admits Joann was a good woman. When Toney went to prison, he offers to help. It was little things like watching Marcus and Yvonne so she could attend college.

Stacy dated Joann for a while. They both agreed to end the relationship. Joann was still in love with Toney, and he was out of jail.

Stacy was one of Toney's homeboys back in the day. He met Toney through his brother Travis AKA T-bone.

T-bone was the one that told the story about the robbery, and how Al Freight left Toney holding the bag for murder.

Travis put money on Toney's books while he was doing time. He also chipped in on the bank account for Toney.

Travis severed his ties with Al Freight after that, and moved to Oakland California. He still keeps in touch with Toney over the years.

Marco has time on his hands to kill before making the run for Al Freight. Trigger and Durango left a couple of hours ago. He was in his apartment alone. It gives him time to reflect on life and the choices he has made.

How did he go from one of the most sought after playas in the city to a brother that is like everyone else? This was not the plan for his life he was not some worthless thug running wild out in the streets.

Marcus chides himself. There has to be away to be free from this lifestyle. His thoughts drift to Alfonzo. He witnessed firsthand a senseless murder of a young man that was not even twenty years old.

No this was definitely, not how he was planning to go out. His cell phone starts to ring. Marcus snaps back to the present, and checks the caller ID before he answers.

He is surprised to see Stacy's name on the ID. What could he possibly want? Stacy was cool with Marcus but very seldom calls. He answers the call.

"What up Stacy?" The voice on the other end sounds serious. "What up Marco man? Look here young brother I need to holler at you. It's real talk man."

Marco looks at his watch he still has a few hours left. "I got you Stacy when and where." The man pauses for one second. "Meet me at Deuces man in twenty." The line goes dead.

Marcus straightens up in his chair. He gets to his feet grabs his jacket and starts for the door. When he makes it to his vehicle, his phone is blowing up again.

He answers the call. It was Gina. "Marcus." He clears his throat then answers. "What up ma?" You could hear her take a deep breath. "Baby what is wrong? I haven't heard from you in a couple of weeks."

Marcus waits for a second before replying. "Gina baby we are good. I am just dealing with some things right now." "Like what Marcus? Please tell me it does not have anything to do with that fool Trigger."

"No baby. Why do you assume it has something to do with Trigger?" "Marcus." She puts emphases on her words. "There is a lot of talk in the streets that Trigger is bragging about taking down some dude named Corey. I believe he has been drinking and your name came up in the conversation."

Marcus was enraged. This was the final straw; he has no more patience left for Trigger. He ponders the information. What was the deal with Trigger? He knows damn well they can catch a case if either one of them are implicated.

His mind begins to race. "Look ma, I am good. Thanks for the heads up Gina. I have to make a run right now. Can we talk about this later?" Her reply is concerned. "Yeah baby. Marcus, be careful." "I got you ma, talk to you later."

He would settle this shit with Trigger in a minute. Right now, he needs to meet up with Stacy. Marcus was there on time as promised. He waits as security pats him down. Marcus enters the club, and tries to let his eyes adjust. The lights are dim and it takes a minute to focus on the next move.

Stacy was sitting at his favorite booth surrounded by his girls. Each woman hands over their earnings for the evening, Stacy spots me coming across the dance floor he motions for me to join him.

Once I make it over to him, I sit down prepared for our talk. He impatiently looks over at the women, and they move from the booth. "Sorry about that young brother. You know a hustler has to keep his game tight."

I agree with the statement then cut to the chase. "I hear you man, but I know you did not call me here to talk about your business. What's up Stacy?"

Chapter 6

Stacy shifts his gaze on me, and takes a puff from his cigar before he replies. "Marco man we need to discuss some things that are detrimental to your health." He pauses for one second. "Word on the street man is that you and your crew are making some noise in the hood."

I sit back in the seat, and drop a hand on my manhood. I was leaning back, and my eyes are on Stacy. There was silence before I answer the question. "What noise would that be Stacy?"

The man gives me an impatient look, before he replies. "Let's be real Marco. You know exactly what noise I am talking about young brother."

He was giving me the opportunity to come clean with him. His eyes narrow. Stacy was waiting on me to come correct. One fleeting moment I wanted to shrug the question off, but I knew Stacy long enough to know he would not let this go.

I hesitate one moment before replying. "Okay you are talking about the little episode in the club a few weeks back." Stacy cuts into me. "You know damn well what the deal is Marco. Why are you trying to play me?"

Stacy replies before I get the chance. "Word is you have been doing some business with the Freights. I know you are grown out here Marco, but I would be less than a man if I did not pull your coat on a few things."

It takes me a moment to get my game back on point, he was asking question that I prefer not to answer. My expression closes. There was no way in hell I was going to give up my crew or myself.

In a calm and tolerant manner, I reply. "That's my business Stacy. I am not up in yours, no disrespect intended." Stacy takes a long sip of his drink, and watches me for a few seconds.

"That is where you are wrong Marco. I helped your mom practically raise you when your father was unable too. That young brother gives me the right to pull your coat. That is real talk."

I could tell I offended Stacy, and that was not my intent. It was better to keep all my dealings on the low. The less people involved the better. "Look Stacy man, I appreciate your concern, but I can handle mine."

Once again, Stacy takes a hard drag on his cigar. When he replies it was sincere. "Marco your dad and my brother Travis thought the same thing. It turns out your dad got saddled with a murder rap and my brother cut all ties with Al Freight."

The man pauses before he continues. "You see Marco your dad and my brother were both crew with Freight. Al Freight was responsible for the robbery and the murder. Your dad went down for a murder he did not commit.

My brother realizes Al Freight would do the same thing to him. Your dad never killed anyone, it was Al and he used your father as the scape goat."

The revelation hit me hard. All these years I thought my father was responsible for a man's death. I sit back in my seat with a look of confusion on my face. My mind was full of questions. Why did my mother keep that information to herself? What really happen?

Stacy could see the confusion on my face and he waits for my questions. I sit up straight in my seat. "Why did my mother withhold this information? And how is it my dad took the fall for Freight?" Stacy takes another gulp of his drink, and crosses his hands on the table.

"Your mom was devastated when your dad was charged with murder. She was pregnant with Yvonne at the time. What choice did she have?

No one would believe hear say over evidence." A somber look crosses Stacy's face. "Your dad's back was up against the wall. He had to provide for your mother and two kids. The sad part is Al knew from the jump that he intended to kill the dealer. Travis and Toney were just a convenience, Al did not care who took the fall as long as it was not him.

Your Mom never knew the whole story. Toney believed it would be better for her to think he committed the crime, and not seek retaliation on his behalf. Understand Marco, Toney loves you kids and your mom enough to let her go on without him."

My chest was tight with emotion, my dad made the ultimate sacrifice. He let my mother walk out of his life because there was no point in her waiting on him with a fourteen-year bid.

I could hardly talk the information made me choke up with emotion. Al caused me to miss growing up with my father in my life and that in my book was unforgivable.

My mind was forming a plan. One way or another, Al freight was going down for all of this. I swear this on everything I love. "So my mother does not know the truth either? Stacy man I cannot explain how I feel about this information, but I appreciate you laying it out on the table. That's real talk."

Stacy looks at Marco with compassion, even though he was a young brother Marco was smart and level headed. "Marco you can count on me man no matter what you have got into, and you know your dad has your back." Marco acknowledges the statement. He never doubted his dad's loyalty.

The problem was he did not want his dad to sacrifice his freedom again. In that moment, he makes the decision to handle Freight and he would do it with his crew. I rise to leave, and then stop to shake Stacy's hand. "Thank you Stacy. You have cleared up a lot of things for me today."

Stacy was watching me with a concern look in his eyes. "Marco, I did not share this information with you, for you to do something stupid. I want you to consider what I have told you and cut ties with Freight as soon as possible."

I look around at Stacy and know the anger was evident in my face. "I plan on cutting ties as soon as possible anyway. The criminal life is not for me man."

The man lifts his drink in a salute. "That's what I want to hear man, you have too much going for yourself to deal with this type of lifestyle, and I know your mother would not want to hear you are involved in any type of foolishness."

I give Stacy a brother man handshake then exit the club. It was time to pick up my boys and roll out to the assigned rail station. My crew greets me as I pull up. We roll out. Once we make our destination, I sit in darkness and wait.

Something was different this time the runners are acting as if they are confused. It was taking too long to open the doors something was wrong here. We exit the vehicle to assist the runners with the doors the next instant spotlights are upon us at once.

I look at my crew we are ready to flee, but our escape is impossible when several police surround the perimeter. I hear officers shouting at us not to move, and the sound of guns ready to fire at any sudden resistance.

To make things worst it starts to rain in heavy sheets that soak us to the bone. The first thing that crosses my mind is my mom there was no way I could avoid telling the truth now.

One officer yells for us to get on our knees with fingers interlocked on top of our heads. This was it everything I worked for was lost with one foolish mistake. My heart is beating a mile a minute, and perspiration is on my lip.

I feel the cold steel of the handcuffs on my wrist, and an undeniable panic sets in on me. The officers drag us to our feet, and roughly place us inside the cruiser.

My boys are in different cars I see officers surrounding my vehicle. Every fake ID I ever had is in the glove box. My mind is moving at a fast pace. Think Marco! You need a way out of this.

I have seen enough cop shows to know what comes next. First, they would take my fingerprints, and a strip search would be next. The one thing I am glad of is there was no weed, which is one less charge to worry about. The ride to the station was one of the longest in my life.

We go to the booking area fingerprints, and empty my pockets all-valuables taken from my possession. This was one bad nightmare, but it was a nightmare of my own making. The flash of light from the camera takes my mug shot.

Here I am looking like some kind of criminal. The image is almost too much to bear. All the while, my mind is roaming over things I could have done better in my life.

I thought about all the games I played, flashes of my childhood intertwined with the memories of my life in the fast lane, and being the player that I was. Instead of concentrating on being the man, my mother worked so hard to bring up. I lost focus and became a victim of the game, it was more important to roll with my crew nothing else mattered.

Look where all of it leads. I am sitting here waiting, and the charges are theft of a railcar and God knows whatever else they want to add to the list. I prepare myself because the next step is interrogation.

Durango sits in the offered chair. The sergeant looks surprised by his calm exterior. One reason Durango is so calm he does not have a record period. The other reason is he has some insurance to help gain his boy's freedom.

The next reason is he wants out of the business association with Freight, and he is sure Marco wants the same. Before he would take a felony or his boys, he would use that bargaining chip.

The sergeant takes a seat. He reaches into his pocket to offer Durango a smoke, and tries the good cop bad cop role first. After that tactic did not work, he switches to hard questioning. The man introduces himself to Durango.

"Mr. Johnson my name is Sergeant Miller you and your friends are in serious trouble. It would be to your benefit to cooperate with us."

Silence greets the man. Durango is staring at the Sergeant with distaste. He is not going to roll on his boys no matter what. In his opinion, Sergeant Miller can keep it moving.

Sergeant Miller attempts to get Durango to reconsider. "Mr. Johnson, I can understand your loyalty to your friends, but the fact remains that you are facing time in prison.

You were caught red handed stealing from a freightliner that is a felony." Durango shifts in his chair he is still defiant unwilling to provide information.

The most annoying thing about this interrogation is this cop was trying to get information and Durango has no use for cops. He never trusted them, and he sure as hell was not going to start trusting them today. His manner is still calm on the outside, but on the inside, he was worried.

The Sergeant is becoming irritated, and calls for his partner. The first thing going through Durango's mind is here we go the good cop bad cop role. *These dudes are a joke.*

Sergeant Miller's partner walks into the room. Miller signals him to join the conversation. The partner introduces himself.

"Mr. Johnson my name is Rafael Ortega. I will not beat around the bush with you. We need information, and I am sure you can provide us with what we need.

We know you are working for someone else this is an organized crime effort. So you see Mr. Johnson it would be your best interest to name the man you are working for, maybe we can strike a deal with the prosecutor on your behalf.

Durango thinks over the information. He was wrestling with himself. He tosses around the idea, but the charges against his crew are the first thing they would have to remove.

Durango shifts in his seat, and then he replies. "I know what you want. You want me to roll over on my boys and that is not going to happen. If you want to make a deal then the first thing you need to do is drop the current charges against my crew and me.

That is the only way I will give you what you are asking for." Miller joins in the conversation now. "What if we offered your friends the same alternative as yourself do you think they would agree to work with us? Durango lifts one brow.

"That depends, Mr. Miller. Are you also offering to drop these charges if we provide you with what you want?" It was Sergeant Miller's turn to pause. *This kid thinks he has the whole scenario figured out.*

"Mr. Johnson if you and your friends are willing to hand over the main man behind this organization the charges against each one of you can be dropped, but you will have to cooperate with us."

Durango shifts in his seat. "Let me think on it. I would like to make my one phone call if that is alright." Officer Ortega is most agreeable. "No problem Mr.

Johnson. Just give us a couple of minutes to talk with your friends."

Durango nods in agreement. He sends up a silent prayer, *"God please let this work."* The two men leave the room. Outside the door, Sergeant Miller has a private word with his partner.

"Looks like we may crack this case after all, judging by Mr. Johnson's reaction he wants out of this situation as soon as possible. Let's hope his friends are as agreeable."

Rafael replies. "I already had a talk with Mr. Davis don't get your hopes up, from what I gathered he is going to hold out till the very end."

Sergeant Miller replies. "We just need to apply a little more pressure. He will break especially if we keep reminding him of his predicament. I have seen tougher men break when their neck is in the noose."

The men continue walking in the direction of the next interrogation room. The door opens slowly and the two men enter the room. Marco is sitting with his hands folded on his chest he looks at the officers when they enter the room. Officer Ortega starts the conversation. "Mr. Harris, it is time for you to make some hard decisions if you want any type of freedom."

Marcus interrupts before Officer Ortega can finish. "Look Officer, I don't have any information that you may find valuable. If you are here expecting me to sell my boys out, then you might as well charge me right now."

The men pull up a chair. Sergeant Miller takes the lead. "You have better think this through carefully Mr. Harris, we have your ID's, and you are being charged with theft of a freightliner. These are serious charges."

Marco's demeanor is cool and unperturbed. *If this dude thinks, he can intimidate me he has another thing coming.* "I have already told you I don't have any useful information." Officer Ortega comments, "that is too bad Mr. Harris, we were about to offer you a compromise that is to your benefit."

Marcus is listing. "And what compromise would that be?" Officer Ortega notices the change in attitude, he has finally struck Marcus interest, and he continues.

"We are willing to work out a deal with the prosecutor to drop the charges if you are willing to help us nail the main player behind these heist."

Marcus thinks on the information. If he agrees, it could take months to prove Al Freight is the mastermind behind this. If he refuses to help then he is facing time and that was the last thing he wants.

He remains detached as he speaks. "What guarantee do I have that you will keep your word?" Sergeant Miller answers. "We would give you something in writing, the case will be dismissed, but you will have to see the assignment through to the end. It might take weeks or months, but you will continue until we have enough evidence. Is that clear?"

Marcus shifts in his seat, and his face carries a frown. "Crystal. If I agree to this, what protection can you provide for my family? We are not talking about some regular person here. This dude has connections all over the city. My life is in danger and so is my family."

Office Ortega replies. "We can move your family if it becomes necessary. We have people on the street that inform us of such things. You have my word that we will provide extra surveillance for your family if you agree to the terms. The decision is completely up to you."

Marcus leans deeper into his chair. "Give me a few minutes to think on this. When do I get to make my phone call?" Office Ortega replies. "Mr. Harris, if you agree to help us with this case, that phone call will not be necessary. You could walk out the door right now just say the word."

Sergeant Miller notices the hesitation, "Let's give Mr. Harris a few minutes. If Mr. Davis is agreeable to the terms, the three of you are out of here tonight."

Sergeant Miller and Ortega rise from their seats. It was time to have a talk with Mr. Davis. The men leave and walk to the next interrogation room. Trigger is half leaning in his seat he straightens up when the men enter the room.

Officer Ortega takes a seat. He places his hands on the table and starts the conversation with Trigger. "Mr. Davis looks like you will go to prison alone. Your friends are ready to make a deal, that leaves you to take the rap."

Trigger looks at the man in disgust. *What did he think he was some kind of stupid chump?* There was no way in hell his crew would ever turn. "Yeah right, is that the best you fools can come up with?" Sergeant Miller stands observing Trigger. He was a cocky little bastard. He waits, as Officer Ortega attempts to get the man to agree.

"I assure you Mr. Davis you will find yourself being someone's bitch in prison, if you refuse our offer." Officer

Ortega pauses to let his meaning sink in. "You can make this easy on yourself or you can go down alone. How do you want it?"

Chapter 7

Trigger begins to panic, beads of perspiration form on his brow. He narrows his eyes. "My boys agreed to your offer?" Sergeant Ortega has a cynical smile on his face. "That's right it looks as if you will be going down alone on this one Mr. Davis, what is it going to be?"

Trigger's mind is racing, maybe it was time to get out of the game, but there would be consequence for his actions, if he dares to cross Freight. It was time to make a decision was he ready to handle the weight of Taft and Max? Images of Alfonzo tear through his mind.

If he stays in the game how long, would it be before Freight takes out vengeance on him? "I will cooperate if you can cut me loose on these charges."

Sergeant Miller responds. "Good, we can accommodate you with the charges, but let's get one thing straight. You will proceed with the plan to the letter, no show boating, and don't get cute."

Trigger nods in agreement. "Give us a couple of minutes to inform our men, and then we will go over the plan with you in the morning."

Trigger's raises his head, and cuts his eyes at the officers. "You are going to hold me in custody even though I have agreed to help you nail this dude?" Officer Miller responds.

"No. we will release you tonight, but you are to meet with us tomorrow, don't worry we will give you and your crew the location." Sergeant Ortega volunteers.

"Just sit tight a few minutes we will get back to you in a couple of minutes."

Marcus is sitting in his vehicle waiting on his boys, the officers kept their word and released them, but not without a price. The car was running. How much longer before they release his crew? Trigger and Durango are walking out of the building.

After the men enter the vehicle, they roll out. Trigger starts the conversation. "Man I thought our ass was gone for sure. I never thought we would have to turn snitch, have you two considered what we are doing."

"Durango answers the question. "Look dude don't start that shit, what other choice do we have? I for one relish the idea of Freight going down. He is a cold hearted bastard."

It was my turn to ask Trigger some questions. "You have time to worry about snitching on Freight. What about your boys?" Trigger was indignant, just what was Marco trying to say? "What the hell are you talking about Marco?"

I was counting to ten trying to keep from tagging his ass. "It means you are more concerned about Freight than your boys Trigger. Yeah homeboy, you have been running your mouth in the street about Corey, and how you took him down. You know damn well that information could implicate all of us."

Triggers temper spikes and he knows exactly where Marco got his information. When he answers the accusation, it is with a sneer. "Okay Marco, now your bitch is running back telling you tales. When I see Gina I am going to beat her ass."

That was the final straw and I snapped. My foot slams on the brake, tires squeal on the pavement stopping the truck in its tracks. My hand is on the door handle.

In one quick movement I shove open the door, and get out of the vehicle. My voice was raw with emotion, and I was yelling at the top of my lungs.

"Bring your tough ass out here Trigger. You are finish disrespecting me. You want to threaten to do my woman harm, fool you must be on the pipe."

Durango and Trigger exit the vehicle, but Durango steps back, and muses. Maybe an ass whipping will make Trigger get it together.

Trigger looks deadly, so arrogant, and sure, that he would be the victor. He takes his time walking over to face me. With his fist closed and eyes narrowed hatred, rage, and vengeance displays on his face.

It was the first time I noticed the envy rise to the surface. Maybe it was always there and I was too blind to see it. He cocks his head to one side and replies.

"You want to take it there Marco? Then bring it, just remember one thing. Your girl is still a lying bitch." That is when I introduced my fist to his mouth. The force of the blow sends him reeling backwards on his ass.

He rushes to his feet and charges me at full speed. I plant my feet firmly on the ground, bracing for the impact. Once he was in striking distance. I hit him hard. The sound echoes in the darkness, and he drops from the force to his knees.

His eyes are wide with disbelief, and rage. When he regains his footing, he releases a strangled noise, and charges again. He was moving fast, and this time my chin snaps back from the force of his fist.

It only stuns me for one moment, and I let loose on his ass forgetting we are friends, today he was a stranger in the streets.

I have him around the neck choking him into submission. The sound of gaging and coughing slices the silence of the night. Trigger lets out a round of curse words, and continues to struggle against me.

When he finally breaks my hold, he swings around to face me with eyes blazing. Our fists fly we both are fighting to prove our manhood.

For the first time in our friendship, we crossed the line, and even I am shocked at the pent up anger driving me.

Our breathing is harsh, but no one will submit. The fight ends after Trigger makes one last attempt to charge me. My closed fists make contact with his jaw, knocking him out, with one solid punch.

Trigger was sprawled on the ground unconscious breathing shallow. After I realize what I done guilt overtakes me. This was my boy, partners for life. We have been through so much together and today the friendship was at its end.

Durango glances over at Trigger unconscious, and lying flat on his back. He puts his hands in his pockets and walk towards me. He replies. "Don't worry about it man. This was bound to happen. Trigger has been pushing you for a long time now. Maybe this will be his wake up call?"

Durango and I walk a short distance before I speak. "Listen man when we finish this with Freight I am considering moving to California with my old man.

This is it Durango, I am done with the game, and tired of running from one chick to the next. There has got to be more to life than what we have been doing."

Durango considers his friends confession, and then he comments. "You know Marco, I feel you on that. Man, I was considering the same thing. Maybe it is time for us to grow up, and have a real life.

Real talk man if we survive this episode with the cops and Freight, my plan is to graduate next month and marry my girl.

On the real Marco, we have two choices, settle down or stay in the game. The worst-case scenario is losing our freedom, or our life. It is just not worth it Marco man."

That was the understatement of the year, but Marco realizes the time was here and now. "Let's take this fool home man." Marco and Durango walk back to where Trigger is out cold and haul him into the cab.

They deposit him at his home, and Marco drops Durango off. Once he was on his own, he drives in the direction of his girl Gina's house. He shuts off the engine in the driveway and calls her phone.

"Hey Gina, baby I'm in your driveway, spend the night with me." She answers in a rush. "Give me a couple of minute Marcus. I'll be right there."

He waits for a few minutes before she opens the car door. She looks at his appearance and instantly knows something was wrong. "What happen to you Marcus?" He notes the panic, and concern in her voice, and attempts to calm her fears.

"I'm okay ma. I just don't want to be alone tonight." Gina considers the information and observes the expression on his face. He was serious. This was the first time Marcus has ever been vulnerable.

She replies. "You don't have to be alone any night baby." They ride in silence. After they enter his apartment, he turns the lights on. Gina stands in front of him. Her eyes roam over his features, accessing him fully in the lite room.

His clothes were soiled and a bruise was on his cheek. She reaches up to touch the area, and without uttering a single word, she leans her head against his shoulder.

Instinct makes him hold on to her, taking comfort in her embrace. A feeling of relief washes over him. At least two minutes pass and Gina remains in his arms.

When she lifts her head to meet his gaze, she licks her tongue over her lips in a nervous jester. He cups her face between his hands forcing her to look at him directly.

What Marcus sees in her eyes is love, and a hunger that surprises him. He draws her deeper into his embrace, as his mouth covers hers. A moan of satisfaction escapes his lips, and he continues to deepen the kiss, tasting every drop of the nectar within her mouth.

Marcus kisses her with a fiery passion. A sense of possessiveness engulfs him after the altercation with Trigger.

His tongue slowly strokes the inside of her mouth igniting pent up passion. The kiss deepens and his arms tighten around her waist, drawing her into him absorbing her strength.

This time the emotion that overtakes him is not lust, or a man playing games, but a man that loves a woman deep down in his very soul.

The emotion was new to Marcus, and it was so potent that he has no choice, but to succumb. This time he was not being the player running game on every woman he could find.

This time was different unique, it was the first time he has allowed love into his life, and the feeling was intoxicating.

Gina could feel his manhood straining against the material, and she continues to hold on to him, as his tongue slowly and deliberately taste, and search her lips.

Need and longing sweeps him away, on a tide of desire moving, his tongue in and out sampling the sweetness, as a bee sampling a flower.

Her moans are soft as he trails light kisses over her throat softly sliding his tongue into her ear nibbling earlobes.

She leans into him exposing herself even more to the onslaught on her senses. Tiny pulses vibrate through her body as strong masterful hands slide further down caressing her skin in a sensual motion, palming her buttocks pressing her even closer against his manhood.

She releases a sharp breath when his tongue roams over one breast touching caressing holding them in his hands. She squeezes her eyes shut as his mouth takes one breast at a time gently circling his tongue on each nipple.

His mind explodes from the sensuality and tenderness of a woman who offers him love without reservation. Tonight proves to Marcus that Gina was very much a part of him.

So much, so that he was willing to defend her at any cost. He abruptly releases a breast, and holds her in his arms. He carries her into his bedroom.

Marcus joins Gina on the bed sliding his body next to her, and taking his time to bring her pleasure like never before.

With her clothes on the floor, he continues to tantalize her senses. The room echoes with sounds of desire, as he slowly touches the fine pubic hairs of her lower half.

His fingers linger in that particular area working his hand back and forth. She moves with the motion, lost in a world of sensuality. Sweat forms on their bodies making a thin sheen, as his lips touch the lobes of her garden.

She squirms surrendering herself to him, as he elevates her thighs to tastes the nectar within. Gina buckles from the sensation of his tongue working magic, and she lifts her head from the pillows tangling her fingers in his hair forcing his mouth further down.

She was climaxing, moaning, and crying out his name. Marcus continues tasting exploring, dipping his tongue in and out of her cave of pleasure.

His teeth nibble at the nub making her convulse moving her hips up and down following the tide of emotion that overtakes her with need.

Her moans are for fulfillment needing him to fill the empty void, but he continues the assault on her senses. Light strokes of his hand touch her as his mouth send pulses racing out of control.

She was at the brink of ecstasy tugging his hair begging for release. He expertly slides his body on top resting between her moisten thighs, and the warmth of his hardness eases into her core.

He was pacing himself. His main goal was to bring her to a full climax, and he succeeds, pushing his hips in and out caressing her garden with the precision of an artist stroking his canvas.

She rides wave after wave of ecstasy, as he continues to stroke her with his maleness pushing her even further over the edge. He was pushing her over the brink of reason, and a confession escapes her lips.

"Oh God Marcus I love you." It was an admission long overdue, and he continues to hold out on his release, more intent on bringing her the ultimate satisfaction.

When he could hold out no more his restraint snaps, and with a roar of satisfaction, his body collapses on top of her shaking with pleasure. He rest between her thighs breathing hard, and exhausted, but for once satisfied.

Finally, he rolls on his side drawing Gina next to his heart. With one arm draped over her waist, she was in safekeeping, and a feeling of completeness surrounds him.

Marcus wakes to the sound of his phone ringing. Once he untangles himself from Gina he picks up the rumpled clothing and search for his cellphone. "Hello this is Marcus."

The voice on the other end was Sergeant Ortega. "Mr. Harris glad I caught you. Just want to confer about the case.

Can you meet me at the hard rock restaurant in about an hour; we can go over the details of your assignment. In addition, we have the runners in custody, so they should not be a problem for you when you do the next run for Freight.

Bring your boys Mr. Harris see you in an hour." Marcus agrees to the terms, hangs up, and run his fingers through his hair. Man it was time to play snitch, but it would also be his ticket to freedom and out the game...

Gina stirs, and her hands deftly search for Marcus, once she realizes he is not beside her. She rolls on one side, and catches a glimpse of him sitting in the chair.

In a lazy voice filled with contentment, she replies. "Come back to bed Marcus, I want to snuggle this morning", she releases a yawn. Marcus snaps out of his train of thought, comes closer to the bed, sits, and leans in to kiss Gina on the mouth.

He murmurs in a low voice while his mouth is still against hers. "You have no idea how much I would love to stay and cuddle with you ma."

It takes every ounce of his will power to pull away from her. When he replies, it is in a strained voice, "I got some work to do ma, but when I return Gina we need to talk about something's on the real."

Gina sits up in the bed, this sounds serious and he has her full attention. "Marcus, is something wrong?" She bows her head thinking the worst, and continues.

"You don't want to see me no more, is that what this is about? Marcus, I thought we shared something special last night." He takes one finger and lifts her chin so they are eye level.

When he answers, his voice is smooth and full of confidence. "Gina its nothing even close to that, ma. Do you honestly think I would have gone there with you, if playing games were involved?

I am serious about us. Gina just trust that we need to talk, and "Gina. —." He pauses for one moment, "I love you ma, on the real."

She was silently holding her breath expecting the worst; slowly her eyes lift to meet his, and tears slide down her cheeks. She sniffs, and then smiles at him, with eyes sparkling with love.

He wipes the tears away with one hand, and claims his rights with her in one smooth motion.

Marcus picks up Durango, and the next stop was Trigger. He silently dreads seeing Trigger today, and hopes there would not be another altercation.

They roll up to Trigger's apartment knock and wait for an answer. Durango pounds louder on the door finally there is an answer. Trigger opens the door to allow entrance, but his eyes still hold resentment. Trigger was sporting a black eye and his lips are swollen.

Marco ignores the look, but notices his boy's bruises. He thinks to himself. *Man*

I messed him up. Marcus gets to the matter at hand. "We need to meet with Officer Ortega this morning, time for this to go down with Freight."

Durango remains silent. He glances between both friends to see what the outcome would be. Trigger walks deeper into the room then reaches for his jacket, when he turns to face his boys, he comments.

"Marco you got a lot of nerve bringing your ass to my house after yesterday." He was glaring at Marco, before Marcus could answer the accusation Durango replies.

"Kill that shit Trigger, You know as well as I do that you have been testing the waters a long time with Marco. If you want to be angry then so be it dog, but this is business put that personal shit to the side."

Trigger looks indignant at his friend, but admits he was right. "Cool man I am with it. Let's roll."

Officer Ortega greets the three young men, and offer to buy breakfast. The men sit down at the table. Officer Ortega leans in their direction looking strange.

With his eyes he examines each man's earlobe, the act was getting on Marcus nerves finally he ask. "Is something in particular you looking for Officer Ortega?"

Rafael Ortega smiles at the men, before he answers. "Yes as a matter of fact there is. I was checking to see if either of you wore an earring."

Chapter 8

The men find the answer strange and Officer Ortega reaches into his jacket pocket, and extracts three jewelry boxes. He slides each man a box. Marcus replies, "I don't know what you got on your mind Officer Ortega, but I don't swing that way." Rafael Ortega burst with laughter, once he gets under control he explains.

"The earrings have a camera inside, and the microphone is on the back clasp. We already expect Freight to be suspicious after the raid of the freight station. He will be looking for a wire and a microphone not earrings."

The men stare at the diamond stud earrings in awe. They would have never guessed technology advanced at that level.

The picture was clearer for each man now. Durango replies. "So we are going to wear the earring when we work for Freight." With a smile, he replies. "This is some double o seven type shit right here. Cool, I am with it."

Rafael Ortega continues to explain how everything works, and what he expects from each man. He goes into details about how they are to contact him as soon as they hear from Freight. It will give his men time to get in position if the situation turns ugly. The men end the meeting with the officer.

Durango waits for Officer Ortega to exit the table then he speaks privately with his crew. "Look here fella's I need to tell you something. I have been holding a recording of Alonzo's execution by Freight. I recorded it on my phone."

My mouth drops open and so does Trigger's. We both ask at the same time. "Why didn't you say anything about that earlier? Durango looks between the both of us.

"I was going to use it to get us out of jail until we were offered the snitch position, and I was not sure if the video was clear enough to use as a bargaining chip." Images of Alfonzo's mangled body appear in

Marco's mind's eye, He shakes his head trying to clear the memory.

Stacy puts in a call to Toney. "What up brother?" Toney was running out of patience, bout time Stacy called. "What's up Stacy? What you got for me?" Stacy pauses for a couple of seconds before he replies.

"Well I put the word on the street about the college boys Marco hangs with, and so far word is the one named Trigger has an attitude problem. He might also be involved in a double murder that took place a couple months back."

Toney waits then probes further. "Do you have anything on Marcus dealings with Al Freight?" There was silence. "Yeah, Toney he's been making runs for Freight. I pulled his coat on a couple of things man."

Toney ask, "Like what Stacy?" "I told him about you Freight, and my brother use to be crew, I also told him what really happen with you doing time for murder.

If it had been anyone else Toney would have been angry, but he knows Stacy used him, as the example to drive his point home to Marcus.

Toney asks. "How did he take the news?" Stacy draws a puff of the cigar. "At first he was angry man. He could not understand why you or Joann kept that from him.

I explained that Joann never knew what happen because you thought it best to keep that from her. I also explained that you made the sacrifice of letting her go on without you."

Stacy hears Toney taking a deep breath. He was still raw from that experience it cost his family, and he harbors animosity with Freight and himself.

He replies. "Stacy man thanks. You did the right thing telling Marcus the truth." Stacy pauses for one moment then replies. "No problem Toney we straight on everything man. What are you going to do now?"

There was silence for a couple of seconds, before Toney answers. "I' am on the nine o clock flight to Chicago man. Stacy I need your silence man.

Do not inform anyone that I am coming to town. I also need you to put in a call to T-bone man. I might need some back-up dealing with Freight."

Stacy was laughing on the line. It was time to handle business the old school playa way. "Count me in man. I am down with you and my brother. I got beef with Freight too."

Toney answers, "Bet, hook that up for me Stacy. I will holler at you when I touch down. Peace."

Toney closes his phone. He was not exactly sure what he was going to do, but to save his son the consequence was not an option.

The meeting with Trigger and Durango ends, and Marcus drops off his crew then drives across town to his mothers. His mind goes over the information Durango supplied and he wonders if they all can truly be free of Al Freight and the game.

He releases a sigh as he pulls into a parking space. He exits the vehicle and rides the elevator to his mom's apartment.

Marcus leans his tall frame against the side of the door. Joann has a welcoming smile on her face seeing her son. "Marcus I am glad to see you son come in."

Marcus leans over to hug his mom then continues inside. Joann looks up at her son and asks. "Marcus can you change the hall light bulb for your mother?"

He smiles and accommodates his mother, after he was finished the doorbell begins to   ring. Joann goes over to answer, and she is double surprised seeing Yvonne and her grandchildren at the door.

After helping them in the apartment, she calls to Marcus. "Your sister and the kids are here." Marcus makes his way to the front room he picks up his nephew, and then his niece.

Yvonne comments. "What up scrub, where have you been? I have not seen you in a while. You do not stop by my house. What's up with that Marcus?"

He makes his way over to his younger sister, who is still a pest and places a kiss on her forehead. "What up sis? How are you? How is Dale doing?" Yvonne looks up at her brother with hands on hips, and reply.

"I am good Marcus can't you tell, and Dale is good. We would be better if you find the time to stop by." Marcus bear hugs his sister. "Stop it. I almost believe you miss me."

She rolls her eyes at him with a teasing smile on her face, and replies. "I do." Joann offers coffee and doughnuts. The children are playing with their toys and, Joann comments.

"What do you want for graduation Marcus? You are running out of time. I talked to your dad he says he will attend."

Marcus has a serious look on his face when he replies. "Mom it does not matter about the gift just having all of you there is enough."

Joann cocks one arched brow at her son. "Well I want to throw you a party or go out to dinner as a family. What do you two think?"

Yvonne answers first. "Let's have it at my house that would be perfect it would give Dale a chance to catch up with Marcus, and we haven't done anything as a family in a while."

She looks at her brother with a sheepish grin. "Which one of your many ladies are you bringing this time Marcus?" His expression changes to something foreign. It was the first time he did not even have to think about the answer.

"Sorry to disappoint sis, but there is only one girl for me these days, and that is Gina." Joann's head snaps around. Was she hearing her son right? Joann is surprised only one woman for Marcus that was a first.

She voices her shock. "My boy is finally growing up. I am proud of you son, it is about time you changed your wicked ways." He laughs at the statement. The day ends well visiting his mother, and sister, but it was time to leave for home.

His cellphone was ringing as he exits the vehicle. Marcus stops looks at the caller ID and sees Al Freight on the line. "What's up Mr. Freight?"

There is a short pause, "Marcus, you have some explaining to do where is my shipment? What happen at the freightliners?"

One thing about Al Freight he was to the point and deadly. Marcus thinks on the question, and comes up with an acceptable lie.

"I have no idea where your shipment is Mr. Freight. The cops were swarming the rail station when we arrived. All I know is it was hot when we rolled up and we left."

Marcus was sweating bullets because he was unable to tell on the phone, if Al Freight bought his story. "I will call you back in a minute Marcus." The line goes dead.

He stands there a few minutes contemplating if he should alert his crew, and Officer Ortega. He makes the call to both his boys and then Officer Ortega.

Officer Ortega informs Marcus to wear the earring, and keep him posted on the next assignment. He looks at the entrance of his apartment building and walks to the elevator. The elevator stops on the ninth floor. As he opens the apartment door with his key, he is curious as to why Gina did not open the door for him.

Once he is inside of the apartment. He is about to call for Gina, but stops dead in his tracks. Gina was there, but she was not alone. The sight before Marcus makes his skin crawl.

Beads of sweat form on his brow when he catches sight of Taft, Max, and Al Freight standing in the room. Gina is sitting on a kitchen chair bound and gagged. He eyes are wide as saucers, and terror is on her beautiful face.

Marcus eases into the room, his eyes never waver from his girl, and the similarity of this scene reminds him of Alfonzo. He chokes down the panic rising from the pit of his stomach. The current scene before him was too familiar, and unsettling.

Al Freight stands in the middle of his living room shifting his eyes from Gina to Marcus. He draws a deep breath then replies. "I would say we have a stale mate here Marcus.

Once again where is my shipment?" My anger is mounting, but I am outnumbered and sure, he would kill Gina without the slightest bit of hesitation. My mind is doing a hundred miles an hour, and I force myself to remain calm when I answer.

"I already told you Mr. Freight the cops were there and we kept going." My eyes are on him looking into those lifeless gray eyes. Al walks over to my kitchen, and run his hands over the counter.

When he turns to face me again, it leaves no doubt he is a ruthless bastard. "Okay Marcus, I have to take your word on that especially since my runners have disappeared.

That could only mean one thing they are in custody. There is another shipment coming in at three in morning. I want you to deliver it to the garage downtown. Taft will give you the address."

Al Freight was walking toward Gina and I move forward blocking his path. Today I would die trying to protect her. Freight abruptly stops in his tracks, and faces me.

He was watching me with hooded lids, and notices the determination in my eyes. A wicked smile touches his lips. "She means a great deal to you. A priceless treasure apparently.

Make no mistake Marcus, if you screw me with this shipment. I will personally come back here and take everything you hold dear." He pauses." I think you already know I don't make idle threats."

His eyes shift over to Max, and he replies in a demanding voice, "cut her loose." He walks towards me and stands only inches away. "Today was another lesson Marcus. Do not think I cannot touch you from a distance. Bring my shipments and all will go well, if you screw me. I will destroy everything around you."

I nod my head after I see Gina is safe, the man and his thugs leave without closing my door. After the men left Gina runs into my arms, she was shaking out of control, and sobbing. In a muffled voice, she replies.

"They forced their way in Marcus. I went to answer the door with the chain hooked. The next thing I knew they broke the chain on the door."

She buries her face in my chest sobbing even more. I try to comfort her as best I can, and then I reply. "Gina you have got to leave my house. I will not have your life in danger ma trying to be with me."

She looks at him shaking her head vehemently. "I am not going to leave you Marcus. The only way I am leaving is if you come with me. You are in just as much danger as me."

How was I going to make a point with that type of logic? She was right. Freight was bold enough to come to my home, and tie up my girl. He is bold enough to kill us both.

My mind is searching every reason to argue Gina's point, but I could not come up with one good excuse.

"Listen to me Gina, this dude is no joke. I have seen him in action he is not averse to taking a life and I don't plan on it being either of us."

Toney's flight is on schedule, and he touches down at Midway airport. He tied up a few loose ends with his business in California. A couple of his partners could handle everything while he was away.

He scrolls through his cell phone dials a cab and puts in a call to Stacy. The phone rings a couple of times before he picks up. "This Stacy, what it is?" Toney smiles, Stacy really needs to get an answering service.

"What up Stacy? You take care of what I asked you?" The man hesitates for one moment. "Yeah Toney, I put in a call to my brother, and he says he's got you Toney.

There is one problem he will not be able to get to Chicago for a couple of days, says he has some business to take care of first."

Toney listens, and then replies. "That is cool as long as I know he will be here in a few it's all good." Stacy asks. "What is the plan man and where are you staying?"

Toney thinks on the question before he answers. "I am staying at the Hilton, and the plan well, we will go over that when Travis arrives."

Stacy replies, "cool, Toney just like I told you earlier brother count me in dog." "I got you Stacy. I appreciate your assistance brother. Let's hook up later this evening have a drink."

Stacy replies, "Bet sounds good give me a call man, peace." His cab is waiting and Toney picks up his luggage and heads out the door.

Marcus makes a call to Officer Ortega. "Hello this is Officer Rafael Ortega." Marcus answers in a rush. "Office

Ortega this is Marcus Harris, look man I had a surprise visitor today.

Al Freight showed up at my place with his thugs, and had my girl bound and tied in a chair. Man I could use your assistance."

Ortega listens intently, and then he replies. "Okay Marcus we can put you up in one of our safe houses, but it might look suspicious. If Freight came by your place today then believe me when I tell you he is having you watched. You will have to monitor everything you do."

Marcus feels like his world is crumbling right before his eyes. He takes a calming breath. "No I don't want to draw any more attention from this dude than necessary.

Can you at least increase the patrols in my area? I am not going to run from my home man."

Office Ortega replies. "I can understand that Marcus, but we want you to be safe, and from what I have read in the report Freight is a master at crime and murder.

I don't want you to risk your neck being a hero." Marcus absorbs the information then replies. "Office Ortega, its going down tonight, at three in the morning he wants me and my crew to make the drop at a garage on State Street."

Ortega hears the concern in Marcus voice, and he feels compassion for the man. This was a dangerous burden, and responsibility for any young man.

"Marcus, don't worry I will be there with my men. We got you covered." Marcus breathes a sigh of relief. "Thanks Office Ortega, that makes me feel a lot better."

He ends the call. Gina waits for Marcus to finish the call, and she tilts her head and replies. "I am not leaving you. Looks like you are stuck with me." Marcus holds his girl closer.

Toney settles into his room, and makes a call to Joann. The phone was ringing. "Hey Toney what are you up to?

Haven't heard from you in a month what is going on?"

The voice on the other end sounds strange, different. "Hey Jo, look baby I need you to do something for me." She was listening. "First don't tell the kids you talked to me and second can you come to my hotel? I am in town and we need to discuss a few important things."

She could not mask the surprise in her voice. "You are in Chicago? When did you get here?" He answers the question. "I got in a couple hours ago. Jo I really need to speak with you in person and remember not one word to anyone not even the kids."

Joann could hear the concern in Toney's voice, but there was something else he sounds worried about something. "Can you give me twenty minutes? I will be there. What is the name of the hotel, and room number?"

After she has the information, it takes her only a moment and she was out the door. Toney pours a drink and waits for

Joann. In his mind, he was working out how to tell her about Marcus and what he fears.

He also decides it is time to tell her the whole story about his prison stay. There was a soft knock on Toney's door. He rises from his seat and goes to answer, Joann was waiting patiently when the door swings open.

She greets Toney with a smile taking in his appearance, and he was as handsome as she remembers. Once she steps inside, he hugs her before he speaks.

"I am glad you could make it Jo. Normally I would not ask you to leave at this time of night, but under the circumstances, I think it best no one knows I am here."

Joann returns the embrace, but she wants answers about the secrecy. "Toney what is going on? Why is it so important that no one knows you are in town?"

He holds her hand and draws her deeper into the room. He needs a moment to buy time, and offers to make her a drink before he replies.

Chapter 9

After she takes a seat with her drink, he sits facing her, and the look on his face is serious. He takes a deep breathe, "Jo, the reason I am asking you not to tell anyone I am in town is because our son may be in trouble.

If what I suspect is true then the only way I can help him is from a distance." Her eyes go wide, and she lowers the drink from her lips. "What type of trouble is Marcus in Toney?" He runs his hands through his hair. When Toney makes that move it was a clear sign to Joann that he was frustrated.

"Jo let me start from the beginning and maybe what I suspect will make more sense to you. He stands and begins the conversation.

"Jo when I went to jail. I left you believing that I killed a man, and that was not the truth. Al Freight shot the dealer and I took the rap. I let you and my children down.

It was also the reason I let you walk out of my life because I did not want you waiting for me with a fourteen-year sentence. The less you knew the safer I could keep you and the children."

He pauses, and Joann cuts in. "Toney why? I would have waited for you. You let our marriage end because you were afraid for our safety. I was your wife Toney, you could have trusted me."

She was hurt, all this time listening to people whispering behind her back and believing some of the things people were saying tore at her heart.

He kneels down and holds her hand, "Jo leaving you and my children was the hardest thing I have ever done in my life. Before you judge me to harshly Jo, take in consideration what I am telling you.

Al Freight is a premeditated killer and our son has gotten involved with him." He reaches up to wipe away the tears running down her face.

"Jo, I thought I was protecting you and my children, please understand.

I talked to Marcus a month ago, and he confessed that he has done some runs for Freight. I was immediately angry. He has no good reason to be involved with Freight.

If my guess is right, Marcus is in the game and you and I know where that can lead. I am here just in case Marcus needs me. I cannot openly help him." He exhales an execrated breath, and drops his head. "I'm a felon Jo."

There was a long silence before Joann answers. "What are you expecting to happen? Toney tell me the truth, are you afraid this Al Freight may harm Marcus?"

He stands and so does Joann. He was searching for the right words, fearing she may panic. "Jo, I am prepared for the worst, remember I grew up with Al.

I am aware of what he is capable of, and so are you." She stares at Toney open mouthed, and her eyes were cloudy with worry. "Oh, no, no, Toney please tell me this is a bad dream. Why would this man want to harm our son? Is it because of you?"

Toney pulls Joann further into his embrace before he responds. "Jo, if Marcus has anything on Freight, or wants out the game the only way that will happen, is if Freight is not breathing. He will not risk his empire, if he feels Marcus is a threat to him.

That is the reason I am here, to make sure our son can walk away without a scratch." All sorts of images were going through Joann's mind. Toney could lose his freedom again trying to protect their son, and Marcus could lose his life if he wants out.

The whole situation was a bleak prospect. She was thankful that Toney was holding her, because she almost collapses in his arms. He feels her knees buckle underneath her, and he guides her to the bed, once he was certain she was okay, he sits next to her.

"What are you going to do Toney? Marcus has missed growing up with his father. Can we go to the police?" she was grasping at straws anything to keep her husband and son safe.

He was holding her on the bed, this was the last thing he wanted for them all. What choice does he really have? He would not sit back and watch his son go down for Al or become a murder victim like the dealer, and god only knows how many other people Al Freight has eliminated. There was a long uncomfortable silence before Toney answers.

He turns to face her on the bed. "Jo, I am from the streets. I have done time in the joint. Our son has done neither, and before I will allow him to follow my footsteps, I will eliminate the problem."

Joann panics her eyes are wide with worry and fear. "No Toney I don't want to lose either of you. Please can we go to the police?" Toney lifts her chin so he could see her face.

"Jo it does not work like that if we inform the police his thugs will return to finish the job. It is like a cancer you have to destroy root of the problem and that is Al Freight."

It was sinking in, and Joann comprehends the situation, what could she do to help protect the two most important men in her life? "Toney I don't want you or Marcus to die."

She breaks down in racking sobs no longer able to remain strong. He holds her in his arms, talking to her in a soothing, voice reassuring her, that he would make this work. He assures her that he would not lose his freedom or their life.

She was calming down numb from the unforeseen danger waiting for her family. She asks in a broken voice." What can I do to help? This is my son too, and I love you Toney, I always have."

The admission of love from Joann was the encouragement that he needed to hear. He places a light kiss on her lips and replies. "I love you too Jo, that has never changed for me not after all these years."

There was a plea in her eyes, and she wipes at the tears. "At least tell me how you are going to help Marcus. Can you manage alone who will help you Toney?"

The look on his face is determined. His eyes are hard but his voice was deadly quite when he replies. "I got this Jo, just trust that I have a plan, and will not be working alone. Our son will be safe, and so will I. Trust in me Jo. I will not let you down."

She snuggles in his embrace drawing strength and comfort. The radio was playing a Teddy Pendergrass song. "Come on go with me."

Toney was having a hard time being this close to Joann. Dam when he inhales the scent of her perfume she smells so good it excites his senses.

Looking at her this very moment reminds him why he fell in love with her in the first place. She was beautiful through and through, and he could not resist the temptation any longer.

He was trying to be cool, not wanting to put a rush on her. After all, he was planning to court her the way a real man does. That was until he was staring into Joann's eyes and she traces her tongue over her lips drawing his attention to her mouth. His eyes could not hide the light of passion, it was evident, but there was something else, it was love.

He lowers his head kissing her with pent up emotions, and she returns the kiss matching his ardor. She craves, needs, and must have him back her life again.

That is why she never remarried in the first place. In her heart, the only man for her was Toney. It was Toney from the very start.

The moment is intense and they both surrender to desire, kissing, touching, and rediscovering each other. Her breathing came in spasms, but she continues to cling to him loving the feel of him against her.

She slowly unbuttons his shirt touching his chest with the palm of her hands. The simple touch makes him gasp almost painfully. How long had he thought about her in his arms? This was his wife, mother of his children, and there would be no turning back now.

He frames her face in his hands, and deepens the kiss searching her mouth extensively with his tongue.

Toney was drowning in a world of sensation. She brought out the best in him, and he continues to let their tongues linger playing with one another. She was enjoying the acts of love with Toney.

He was the father of her children, and love of her life. Only he could open her heart to love. He abruptly breaks the kiss off needing confirmation that this is what she wants.

"Jo, are you sure you want to take it there." She was breathing erratic but replies. "We already have and yes I want to take it there with you."

That was all the confirmation he needs and he loves her with a ferocity that leaves her breathless, and wanting more, After the loving was over Toney replies.

"Jo this was everything I imaged and more. You know I am not going to let you get away again right." She kisses him with left over passion and replies. "Good because I am here to stay Toney. This is where I belong with you and our children."

The evening passes with Joann and Toney snuggled in each other's arms, both looking forward to a future together.

Al Freight was not a man easily deceived, and he questions Marcus account of the raid at the freightliner. No, something about Marcus's story just did not add up and he was going to make sure Marcus was on the up and up.

He sits in his large office chair and calls for Taft. The man enters Al's office he was big as a barge, and asks as soon as he enters the office. "You want to see me Mr. Freight."

Al instructs Taft to take a seat, as he lights his cigar. Freight takes a deep pull from the cigar before he replies. "Yes Taft I need you to do some investigating for me, it concerns me about the raid on the freightliner."

The man Taft replies. "What you have in mind boss? You smell something foul with the runner's story." Freight takes another deep pull from the cigar. "I did not make it this far not covering my bases; the one named Marco is the son of Toney Harris.

Even though Toney did some time on my behalf I am not certain his son carries the same characteristics." Taft sits back in the chair with his large hands on his lap.

"What you need me to do Mr. Freight?" Al's gray eyes became slivers, "I want you to check on one particular runner that was at the freight station that night.

His name is Robert Turner, and he has been in my employ a long time. I know he is loyal visit him at the jail ask him if Marco and his crew showed up when the cops arrived or did they simply leave as he says.

Once you have that information I will decide how we will handle the problem." The big man's face splits into a smile. One thing Taft enjoys is killing and it would be his pleasure to eliminate any threat to his boss or organization.

"How soon you want me to make a visit to Robert?" Al Freight thinks on the matter before he replies. "Make it as soon as possible Taft. If Mr. Harris is setting us, up. I want to know about it, believe me he will never betray anyone else."

Taft was all for killing Marco and his crew, if he had his way about it, they would have died alongside Alfonzo. "I will get right on that Mr. Freight is there anything else?" Al looks at his man Taft.

"Just start there Taft I will keep you informed." The big man named Taft gets to his feet, and leaves the office. AL was still sitting in his chair, making plans to eliminate any loose ends.

Marcus wears the earring, and so does his crew. He takes a deep breath trying to remain calm and emotionless, and waits in darkness as the runners use the bolt cutters on the doors. Once again, he pulls up to load the inventory. Taft mentioned that Mr. Freight's item was a Maytag dishwasher, and includes the model number, but not the contents.

Marcus already knows he is delivering drugs and is more determined to leave the game. On this night, all goes well, without any problems. They make the drop and go home. He continues his duties with school and work, taking each day at a time waiting to get enough information on Freight.

Meanwhile Toney goes to meet with Stacy and his friend Travis (T-bone) they have a lot to catch up on, and Toney was ready to lay out his plans for the Freight family. It was time to bring Al Freight down to his knees.

The three men meet at the hotel. Toney was being extra careful covering his tracks with every move. He is more determined than ever to get Marcus out the game, and start a life with Joann. Travis is five feet nine with a sturdy build, and pure muscle. Travis and Stacy rise from the bar to greet Toney as he comes near.

"What's up man, it's been a long time dog. How you living man?" Toney greets his boy it has been too damn long, and the worst part about, it is they have to meet under these circumstances. Toney shakes Stacy's hand, and greets his partner.

"What up Travis. You looking good man I see life has been good to you brother." The men sit at the bar and Toney begins the conversation. "Look here brothers the reason I asks you to come to Chicago, is I need your assistance."

Travis notes the concern in his friend's voice, and observes the stress and the agitation. It must be a serious matter for Toney to be contacting him sounding worried. Stacy mentioned Al Freight and Travis knows there is beef with these two, maybe Toney was ready to settle the score with Freight. Travis sits back prepared to hear the rest of Toney's conversation.

Toney continues. "Man you know there is no love loss on me and Al's part, but this involves my son man. He has got in the mix with Freight." Toney pauses. "In addition, you know he cannot just walk away from the game without consequence. I need to handle Al man. Are you both with me?"

Travis leans just a little in his seat. He was expecting this from Toney it was not a surprise in the least. He looks directly at his boy. "I got you. Toney, just tell me when and where man I am there."

Stacy nods his head then replies. "You already know I got you Toney."

Toney breathes a sigh of relief. He guessed correctly Travis was still his boy after all these years the friendship was still stronger than ever. Travis and Stacy notice the relief on Toney's face.

It was time to ask the main question. What was the plan of action? He puts this question to his friend. "What do you have in mind for Freight Toney? I need to know how you want to handle this business. Of course we trust your judgment bro, and we know you got to have this to the letter, so what is up man?"

Toney thinks on his boys question he waits for the bartender to finish serving their drinks before he answers the question. "Here it is brothers. My plan is to drop in on Al unannounced, but before we can do that, I have to start tailing my son.

I need to see where he is conducting business. The plan is to wait for Marcus to do another run for Freight then come up in his spot and demand he let my son out of the game.

We all know he will not and that is when I will put his ass six feet deep. No, looking back man you feel me on that?" Travis raises one brow at his friend, and takes a deep swallow of the alcohol, before he replies.

"I will be the first to agree with you on this Toney. If it was my son I would take the same measures, but make sure we got this down man because you don't need to go down again for this fool."

Stacy provides input. "Look here brothers. I am down with whatever you two want to do. Freight has caused problem for me plenty of times. It's time to x this fool out."

Toney nods in agreement. The three men talk for several more hours and decide how to clean up their mess. With Freight out the way, no other innocent person would ever have to fear leaving the game.

Taft makes his rounds to the county jail after confirming the visitor dates with an officer. He sits in the visiting room, and waits for inmate Robert Turner. Ten minutes later the man appears looking for his visitor.

Taft waves the man in his direction picks up the receiver, and waits for him to do the same. Robert looks confused. He was expecting one of his family members, or Mr. Freight to bond him out not Taft. The man stares from behind the glass divider and waits for Taft to begin the conversation.

"Hello Mr. Turner, I assume you were not expecting me, and that is fine. I was sent here by your employer to ask some relevant questions."

The man interrupts. "Yeah man that is all good, but when are you going to bond me out of here?" Taft ignores the question and continues. "I need you to answer a couple of important question then we can discuss your bond.

The man shakes his head in agreement, and replies. "Okay what do you want to know?" Taft leans forward as if to share a secret. "There were supposed to be three runners to haul the freight the night of the raid.

Do you remember them being at the freight station or not." The man thinks on the question before he answers. "Yeah I remember those brothers, and know them from around the way man. They came to help us with the doors on the freightliner.

I am positive the three men were there because five-o placed them in a car. Now that you mention it man, I have been in custody a couple of weeks now and have not seen one of them in here."

Taft leans back in the seat this is the information that his boss was looking for. He directs his attention to the man behind the glass.

"Good job Robert. Hold tight I will let our boss know that you were very helpful and loyal. He will make bond for you."

The man nods in agreement he leaves for his cell, and the visit was finished. Taft smiles at the thought. Looks as if he would get to do what he does best killing, and he would enjoy every minute hearing the three men scream in agony.

The next day Joann continues to pay visit to Toney. She was looking forward to a life with him once Marcus was safe. Today for Marcus is going slow. At work, he has to deal with Carol trying to get another date, but this time he puts his foot down with her.

There was not going to be anything between them except a work environment. He was still receiving calls from different honeys but that was about at an end with Marcus also.

Chapter 10

Life was short and he was not about
to spend his chasing females, no this time he
was sure a life with Gina was at the top of
his priorities. His boys want to go out
tonight, but Marcus refused. He was going
to a club and dinner with Gina tonight.

With all the drama hanging over his
head, a night out with his girl was just the
ticket to relieve some stress. He leaves work
and drives home. Once Gina was ready, they
leave for a night on the town. The evening
was going good. They have dinner and then
go to one of Chicago's hot spots.

It was a laid-back atmosphere, and
they bump into Stacy at the club. Marcus
makes the introductions and introduces
Gina. Stacy gives Marcus a brother-man
handshake, and whispers in a low voice.
"Hang on to her man she is fine."

Marcus hit him up with another
handshake and turns to go to the dance floor

with his girl. The sounds are mellow, that old school R&B the kind that put couples in the mood for love.

I hold Gina in my arms as we slowly move to the music. She leans into me, and my hands grip her curvy body. I bend my head inhaling her perfume and place light kisses on her neck. We are so into each other that I never noticed the girl named Brenda approaching. Gina was slow grinding her body against mine, and we are so close that I am sure she feels my errection through her material...

My hands slide against her body running both hands up and down a firm backside in sensual motions. She was making me want her even more. Just as I lean down to tongue, kiss her someone was tapping my shoulder.

My face carries a frown because whoever is tapping me is interrupting my game. When I swing around to face the intruder I am staring at Brenda, and she is pissed off.

Stacy finds a seat and puts in a call to Toney and Travis. He was informing Toney of Marcus activities. The girl named Brenda rolls her eyes at Gina, and starts making accusations.

"So Marcus you can lay up with me, but you cannot call me. I am beginning to see why, guess you call yourself some kind of playa." She looks at Gina again rolling her eyes. Marcus separates himself from Gina for one brief moment. She was standing beside him. Then his temper takes hold,

"Look here ma. You were a one-night stand, you feel me. Do not come up in here acting like it was anything more. Your best bet is to keep it moving, you feel me."

The girl is clearly irritated and the scent of alcohol was strong in the air. Brenda becomes reckless. "What you trying to say Marcus? That I did not make you call out my name when I was putting it down on your ass. You can stop trying to front for your bitch."

That was it, and he loses patience with the woman. Marcus was not the type to hit a female, and not about to start today. He gets a grip on his temper and tries to ease the situation. "Brenda, why are you tripping? I never made you any promises, and you knew what the deal was. Fall back ma, and stop insulting my girl. You need to check yourself, and quit trying to make more out this shit than it is ma." Gina is standing next to Marcus in disbelief.

Gina knew that Marcus was unfaithful, but like a fool, she chose to hold on. What did she expect from him anyway? *Maybe some loyalty, love, and trust.* The woman admits she is making a fool of herself. She muses, just another lying ass brother running game on women I 'am done with this shit.

She sends another nasty look over at Gina, and a "fuck you Marcus." Then she was ghost. Marcus already knows drama is on the way with Gina, and he tries to smooth things over.

"Gina before you go in the wrong direction let me explain. I slept with that chick way before we decided to be committed. He pauses to look her directly in the eyes.

"Gina when I said I love you ma, that was real. I have changed baby and that is real talk." He was so sincere she has to ask. "Are you telling me that you are done with the game Marcus? Because I for one hope so, I want a life with you baby."

He draws her into his arms on the dance floor, and puts his lips against hers kissing her with passion, intensity, and love. A couple of days later Taft was entering Al Freight's office the big man takes a seat before he replies.

"I got that information you asked for, had a talk with our runner Robert Turner. He informs me that Marco, Trigger, and Durango where at the freightliners the day of the raid."

Al Freight slams down his fist hard on the desk. His eyes were slits and a crease forms on his brow. "That son of a bitch, got the nerve to fuck with me? He leaves his desk to pace and Taft adds fuel to the fire.

"The runner also tells me that the three of them never were incarcerated. He says they have not done one day in jail, and that could only mean one thing. They are snitches."

Al rubs his hand against his cheek, before he replies. "And we both know what happens to snitches. No one fucks with me. I told that bastard there would be consequence, if he fucked with me. It is time to make good on my promise."

Taft leans forward in his seat. "How do you want to handle this boss?" Al's lifeless gray eyes never falter. "Call Max we have a special delivery for these three only this time they won't walk out alive."

A wicked smile touches Taft's face it was time to kill again and he loved it. Al continues. "We are going to perform a strip search on their punk asses. Do not leave anything. That includes jewelry, clothing nothing on their bodies.

If they are working for the cops, believe me they are wired. I do not want you to miss anything search every crevice. Then we will give them a fake location, but this time they will be leaving unexpectedly with us. We can take it from there."

Toney makes good on his promise and follows his son. Travis and Stacy ride with him each man knows the trip will end with death but the bond is strong, and so is their loyalty.

The men will ride it out to the end. Joann was leaving work about to get into her car, when a large man approaches her. The hair on the back of her neck stands up, and she has an uneasy feeling, but she swallows down the panic. She frantically looks around maybe she could scream for help. In her mind, this was a common mugger, but in reality, it was Max waiting to abduct her.

Just as she is about to scream for help a hand covers her mouth stifling the sound. The big man forces her into the car intensifying her fear. She becomes even more afraid when Max shoves a gun against her ribs.

At that moment, she becomes limp and stops resisting. The man barks at her in a commanding voice. "Good move. I would hate to kill you because you were being difficult."

Joann's eyes go wide with fear and screams of terror invade her mind. What is going to happen to her? God, no one even knows she is missing... This is the first time in her life that she has ever been completely helpless.

Who would help her now? The large man climbs into the driver's seat, but keeps the gun aimed in her direction. Joann hears the door locks engage, and the motion of the car as the man drives out the parking lot.

Meanwhile Al Freight calls his man Max to ensure he has succeeded in capturing Marcus's mother Joann. Once Max confirms he has her in tow. Al makes the call to Marcus.

The phone rings a couple of times before Marcus picks up. "What up Mr. Freight." Al has a wicked look on his face as he grips the phone trying to restrain anger.

In a calm voice, he replies. "Marcus I want you to listen very carefully. If you fuck up believe me it is going to be costly to you. I know you are working for the cops--."

There was a pause. "Marcus, I have someone near and dear to your heart. My advice to you is not to try any shit. You hold tight I will call back in a few moments. Your best bet is to stay by the phone." Taft sits in the parking lot waiting on Marcus.

As soon as Marcus walks toward his car, Taft exits his vehicle. He bolts toward Marcus moving with agility. Before Marcus has a chance to react, the big man is on him, choking him out in the parking lot.

Marcus knew the first time he met Taft that he was nothing but a killer, and fear covers him like a cloak. Marcus was trying to break the hold around his neck, but this dude's grip is like a vice and he cannot budge him.

Toney is watching the attack on his son in horror. His hand reaches for the door, ready to make a move to help Marcus, and

Travis stops him. "Hold on Toney, he is not going to kill Marcus in the open there are witnesses.

He is trying to scare him. Hold up man." Stacy has to restrain Toney before he blows their chance at Freight. Stacy replies. "Toney, hold on brother, I know this is difficult to watch, but hold steady man." The scene goes on for a couple of minutes, but in Toney's mind, it was hours. Marcus is still scuffling with Taft refusing to give up even though the man is like a mac truck.

Once Taft gets Marcus under control, he speaks. "Listen to me, you and I are going to meet up with your friends. You understand." Marcus nods his head.

Taft takes out his cell phone and places a call to Max. He was giving his location. Max agrees to meet Taft at Marcus's work place, and then they would leave together.

Once the other man arrives, Taft forces Marcus back into his truck. Max sits in the back with Marcus at gunpoint. He waves the gun in his face.

With the barrel aimed at Marcus, the big man orders him to call his boys. Taft drives off with Marcus and picks up his boys. The next stop was an old abandon building. Taft and Max force the men out the vehicle and make them strip down nude. Taft is adamant he orders Marcus and his crewmembers remove every item jewelry, clothing, and shoes.

Once the men are in the raw Taft searches them fully. He makes them spread butt cheeks, and performs a search. This was the most humiliating episode in Marcus life.

Max gathers up the items tossing them in the corner. Then Taft makes the call to Al Freight. "All clear we have them where to Mr. Freight?" Al orders his men to bring Marcus and his crew to the abandon warehouse on one-hundred sixty- eighth where Joann resides.

The men return to the vehicle driving at a high rate of speed. Toney and his crew are still tailing Marcus and his friends. Toney is worried after witnessing the strip down of Marcus and his friends.

It becomes clear to Toney that Marcus's crew is on the snitch list, and Freight would definitely eliminate his son. Marcus and his crew accept reality their life is about to come to a terrible end.

Reality came crashing down with all three men. Without the earrings, there is no way to contact Officer Ortega. Marcus never thought about his life ending in this way, but today the possibility is too real, and this time he was afraid.

An abandon building comes into view from what Marcus could tell they are on the North side of town. A chill covers his body and he shivers from having no clothing, and the fear of dying.

Taft points his gun in their direction and yells. "Get your asses out, looks like it is time to wear that mob necktie for your disloyalty." Durango and Trigger know time is up for all of them.

We get out of my truck nude, as the men shove the gun at our backs. We move toward the garage type doors and it opens. Standing in the mist was Al Freight looking like the murdering bastard he was. As we move further into the building, I notice movement in the corner of the room and my mouth drops open.

It was my mother bound and gagged in a chair scared out of her mind. Al points the gun at my mother looking between the two of us. "Marcus I told you, if you fucked with me that I would take away something near and dear to your heart.

What could be dearer than your mother?" The bastard points the gun directly at my mom, and I react. The next thing I know is I was naked, diving on this big man knocking him to the ground, and the gun slides across the floor.

Max was rushing over to try to help Al and Durango manages to jump on his back. Durango was pounding his fist against the man's head, but the blows do not faze Max.

The big man shakes off the blows with strength, and reaches for Durango. He grabs his head and slams him to the ground. Trigger makes a beeline for the gun that slid across the floor, but Taft has a pistol to the back of his head.

My dad and his crew are shocked at the scene before them Toney takes an unsteady deep breath after he catches sight of Joann tied in the chair and Marcus on the ground butt naked scuffling with Freight.

Stacy aims his gun at Taft's back, and the man drops his weapon. Travis has his gun on Max forcing him to release Durango. My dad yells at me to move out of the way.

I roll off the big man and Al Freight gets to his feet. Toney was deadly standing face to face with Al Freight. The man cuts his eyes at my father and his mouth twist with a sneer. Raw hatred was in his eyes, and Toney is murderously angry forcing himself to speak.

"This is how you repay me Al by taking out my family." Al's lifeless gray eyes are cold devoid of any type of emotion. He cocks his head to the side and replies." I spared you son's life once. I will not spare it again. Consider my debt paid in full."

The words rang out in Toney's ears, but the decision to eliminate Freight was a done deal. This would be the last time Al and Toney would meet. Toney eyes slide to Marcus and his crew. In a voice tight with controlled fury, he orders Marcus to release Joann.

Once he satisfied that Joann is safe, he asks Marcus to take his mother and crew away from the area. Marcus hesitates leaving his dad. "Dad, please I don't want you to lose your freedom. Call the cops and let them handle this please."

At this point Marcus was going to try anything to keep his dad a free man, even pleading with him. Toney was not going to live his life looking over his shoulder and neither was his family. Toney accepts the consequence of his actions, and prepared to go back to prison for his family if necessary.

The possibility of a conviction for Al was slim in chance. The only way to put the past to rest was to eliminate Freight. In a firm voice, Toney answers Marcus. "Son, take your mother home and leave the area now dam it."

Marcus does what his father asks. Joann attempts to stop Toney fearing she would lose him forever. "Toney please don't do this we are okay." Marcus has no doubt his dad was going to finish the job. Marcus places one arm on Joann's shoulder guiding her away from the building.

After Toney was sure, his family and Marcus friends were clear of the area. He makes one last attempt at conversation with Al. "Did I hear you right Al? Your debt is paid. You motherfucker, I rotted in jail for your bitch ass and you try to kill my son, and his mother. I will see you in hell."

Toney takes a couple steps toward Al, lifts the gun and pulls the trigger. The building echoes with a loud bang, and the bullet lodges in Al's head. The man drops to the floor with a thud. Al died with his eyes open staring at Toney. Stacy and Travis take out Taft and Max, it was over, finally over and the men disposed of the bodies never to look back at this again.

After it was finished Toney gives his partners dap and the men separate. Marcus knew his father was going to kill the men. He was not sure how he should feel, but admits his dad killed the men to protect his mother and him.

After Joann, Durango, Trigger, and Marcus reach the vehicle. They drive away from the abandon building, and Marcus drops off his boys. He was driving his mother home.

It was very embarrassing to walk up to an apartment complex in the raw, but he manages. Once he collects something decent to wear. He sits down to talk with his mom. She is shook from this episode and I put my arms around her shoulders, and try to comfort her. My mom reaches for my hand and places it against her cheek, as tears stream down her face.

Her voice is shaky when she speaks. "Marcus son, I thought I lost you. I am glad you are safe, now let's just pray your father is okay." I could tell my mom was worried about my dad. It was clear to me that she still has love for him, and the possibility of my parent's getting back together makes my heart jump for joy.

I was pacing, waiting at my mother's for word from my father. Just when I was about to call the phone rings. It was my dad on the way over. When Toney arrives at Joann's Marcus greets him at the door.

Toney's face is strained with guilt his conscience, replaying the scene taking out Al Freight, but he has to live with it. Toney smiles at his son and hugs him tight. Marcus and Joann's safety were worth it, and he has no regrets. Joann hurries into Toney's arms holding him laughing and crying at the same time. Toney embraced his wife and promise not to ever let her go.

Things were starting to calm down after a couple of weeks. Joann was beginning to fall back into her routine, and she continues to see Toney. Gina and I are working things out in our relationship.

Man that was a new word for me "Relationship" since I use to be the one who avoided commitment at all cost, but today it is what I crave the most. My boys are doing well since the episode with Freight.

Our graduation was less than a week away, and it seemed that life got even better, after we left the game. Until Sergeant, Ortega called my phone. I was so busy trying to get back on track and normal that he never crossed my mind.

The phone was ringing and I answer. "Hello." Apprehension was in my voice. The man on the line responds. "Marcus this is Sergeant Ortega. I am checking in with you haven't hear a peep out you in a couple of weeks what the stats on Freight?"

I swallow hard, before I answer. "How are you doing Office Ortega? I have not heard from Freight, since the last run. I don't know what's up." Marcus lies to cover up the business with Freight.

Chapter 11

Officer Ortega releases an execrated breath. "That is strange Marcus, one minute you're on the phone scared for your safety. The next you have not heard a word from him." Marcus was holding his breath hoping the officer would buy the deception.

He probes a little further. "Where do we go from hear Officer Ortega? We kept our end of the bargain." Officer Ortega admits the men did do as asked, but he wonders how his partner would take the news that Freight may have skipped out on them.

Officer Ortega answers the question. "Well Marcus it seems that we may not have a case to prosecute. If Freight has stopped contacting you, then it leads me to believe he has left town. I won't keep you Marcus have yourself a good night." Marcus releases his breath and replies.

"Thanks Officer Ortega." Marcus ends the call. Trigger was enjoying his freedom and the fact that all of his crew made it out safe. He was chilling at the club when a man from around the way approaches him.

The man is hesitant at first Trigger was known for coming unglued on brothers. He squares his slim shoulders and makes his way towards Trigger. "What up dog long time no see man?" Trigger stares at the man for one moment then memory catches up.

He remembers the man goes by the name Bass. He acknowledges the man, "What up Bass. What you doing up in here? The man takes a seat before Trigger offers. He was looking around as if he did not want anyone to hear what he was about to say.

Then he proceeds. "Look here Trigger man. I don't know if you are aware of it man, but there has been a couple of cops asking a lot of questions about you, and your crew man."

Trigger puts his hand on his manhood, leans back in his seat, and then looks at the man directly. "What kind of questions are they asking man?" The man named Bass looks nervous. He clears his throat, "well first off man. I wouldn't ask, but I need a few dollars for the information man." Trigger tosses him a twenty then looks impatient. The man swallows hard again and continues. "They want to know about a double murder that took place a few months back man."

The man looks anxious and continues. "I did some checking man. The dude the cops are asking about is Corey, and one of his boys. From what I gather the third dude survived and he can identify you and your crew man." Trigger leans further into his seat.

The information about takes his breath away, but his face remains unreadable. "Damn, alright man good looking out." Trigger rises to leave then pauses. "Look here Bass keep me informed man.

There will be something in it for you." The man hurries away from Trigger, smiling at the quick twenty he just made.

Trigger was not prepared for this news. His graduation was right around the corner.

It was just his luck. When he decides to change, here comes new drama to knock him down again. He goes over every detail of the conversation with Bass and there was only one solution.

There was no way he would ever get close to the witness. The police have him under protection. If he does not admit to the murder then his crew's future is lost. Man he owes Durango and Marco that much. He has to break the news to his crew. Trigger makes the call to his crewmembers. He asks them to meet with him on fifty-First Street a small neighborhood club.

He was having a drink at the bar when his boys enter the establishment. Trigger leaves the bar to meet his boys. The men sit together in a booth after doing their handshake.

Trigger starts the conversation. "Hey fella's glad we all are here after the deal with Freight. Look man I will cut to the chase. I got word today that five-o is asking questions about Corey and his boys—." He pauses, and Marco and Durango eyes go wide not expecting this to come back.

Trigger continues, "look fella's, I know I was not as down with you brothers or a good best friend, but real talk man. We are crew and that is something you cannot throw away no matter how hard you try." He runs his hands through his hair, and then looks at his friends with a serious expression on his face.

"Man I will take the heat for the murders man. I just got word that one of Corey's crew survived. He is in police protection. This dude can ID all of us, and you brothers have been down with me from the jump. I owe you that at least."

Durango asks. "Man you sure about this man we are talking a lot of time man." Trigger replies, "What is the alternative man? If I don't step to the plate you two will fall with me." He shakes his head in disgust. "No dog. I have put my boys in enough jeopardy making stupid moves. I got this man."

Marco's respect for Trigger skyrockets. Trigger never thought of anyone but self and today he proves to Marco and Durango how loyal he is to his crew. "Trigger man, I don't want you to take the fall man we all played a part in this."

Trigger stares Marco in the eyes, and replies. "You and I Marco since we were knee-high dog, but I cannot let you brothers fall man. It was my ideal to kill that brother not yours. I got this man." Today was the first time in our association that we learned something new about our boy Trigger.

All these years he has put on a front wild, reckless, and uncaring that Trigger we were use too, not this dude that is ready to sacrifice his life to save ours. I stand and hug my boy. "Trigger you know we won't desert you man. That's real talk brother."

We all do our handshake and leave going in different directions. The week of graduation was here. My parents are proud of their son and the two of them are still dating. I look at them wondering how long it will be before my old man asks my mother to remarry him. A smile touches my lips, because I am glad to see them together again. The day of graduation, was a daze for me. When I attend the ceremony, and look over at my parents beaming with pride, hell even I was proud of myself.

I had finished college ready to tackle the world. My sister Yvonne gave a party for me at her place. I sit and mingle with my girl and our parent's. The night was going well my boys attend they were having a good time. I glance over at my parents they were slow dancing and laughing.

It was a good feeling that I want to last. I hold Gina's hand drawing her towards the dance floor. Then I put my head against her neck to snuggle up closer. She replies. "Marcus I like this new side of you baby. Please don't change a thing."

I smile down at my shorty. Yeah I could say that with pride finally there was only one girl for Marcus Terrell Harris. I whisper in her ear. "Gina I am straight ma, no changes this is the real Marcus. I been thinking baby maybe it is time to consider taking this a step further."

Her eyes go wide on me, and I never release her from my stare. My hand fumbles with my jacket for the box with her ring. When I grasp it securely in my hand, I reply. "Ma, I want to marry you, but first we need to be engaged, if you will have me Gina I want to be your man." She lets out a loud gasp, and her eyes shine with tears. The answer stumbles out of her mouth. "Yes, yes, yes Marcus. Baby this is the happiest day of my life Marcus.

She presses her lips to mine and I accept her love without any reservation. Sergeant Miller is not happy with the results of the Freight case. He planned on is promotion from this case and now all was lost.

He sits back in his chair and muses. Why did freight give up without a fight? What am I going to do about the new allegations against Marcus and his crew? He looks at the warrant on his desk half dreading that he would have to be the one to serve it on Marcus and his crew.

He shakes the misgivings hell he was the law it was his job to see justice served.

His thoughts cease when Officer Ortega enters his office. Ortega pulls up a seat looks at the warrant on the desk, and begins the conversation.

"How you want to handle this Miller?" He points at the warrant. Office Miller shrugs his shoulders. "You sure our boys were involved in this murder Ortega?" Officer Ortega looks Miller square in the eyes.

"According to the witness all three men took shots at the victims. He mentions that Marcus Harris gun fired by accident during their scuffle. So he is the only crew member that did not have intent." Miller thinks over the information before he replies. "Well looks like we need to pick all three men up tonight.

There is no need to wait any longer, and maybe we can surmise what really went on with these three." Ortega did not like this one bit. Just from the short time knowing Marcus and Durango they just did not fit the MO of a killer.

Now Trigger on the other hand was what he would expect. Everything about him reeks of thug right down to his demeanor. He was cocky and arrogant, the typical gang banger. Ortega voices his thoughts about the men to Miller. Miller replies. "Don't get your panties in a bunch Ortega. We will get the man responsible. If the other two are innocent then it has to be the one named Trigger."

The officers leave to make the arrest of Marcus and his crew. The party was still going on when the officers arrived at the house. Yvonne alerts her husband that the police are at the door. Dale speaks with the officers a couple of minutes then allows them entrance.

Toney was in mid conversation with Marcus when he notices the officers approaching their circle. Marcus follows his line of vision and sees the officers on their way towards him and his crew. His mind is full of unanswered questions. *What are Officer Ortega and Miller doing here?* Man this cannot be happening. Officer Ortega walks into the circle and reads Marcus his Miranda rights, before he puts the cuffs on.

Joann and Toney are outraged both demanding answers from the authorities. Toney's voice was a loud roar. "Just what are you doing? What's the charges officer?" Officer Miller explains to the family that Marcus and his friends are being charge with double murder.

Toney's mind is moving fast there was no way anyone would know about Al Freight he cancels that from the list. No, it has to be something else. He asks his next question. "Who was murdered? And what does it have to do with my son and his friends?"

Officer Miller was becoming irritated with Toney, and his answer is curt. "Mr. Harris I understand you are a concerned parent, but please let us do our job. Your son was involved in a double murder, and we have a surviving witness that will testify to the allegations."

A loud gasp escapes Joann. This was unbelievable there is no way her son would be involved in something like this. No way in hell, she raised Marcus better than that, she takes a hard look at her son in handcuffs and wonders if she knows him at all. With a plea in her eyes, she walks closer to her son and asks needing him to deny the allegations. "Son please, is any of this true? Marcus did you have anything to do with a murder son please."

Gina was trying to hold on to Marcus tears streaming down her face. She was waiting for his reply also. Marcus was going to admit his role in the incident, but Trigger answers for him. "No. Marcus and Durango were not involved in any murder.

It was all me let them go Officer they did not have anything to do with this. I am the one who wasted these dudes." I look at my boy making the sacrifice with a look of defiance cocking his head to the side going out like a G. We make eye contact my boy gives me a sign that says it is all good, and I go along with what he says so does Durango.

The officers release Durango and me. After Trigger confesses, they place him in cuffs, and practically drag him away. My mom breathes a sigh of relief and so does the rest of my family. The expression on my dad's face alerts me that a serious talk was on the way.

When my family was sure I was not leaving in handcuffs, my dad calls Durango and me over to talk. His hands are deep in his pockets and he was pacing, and then starts the conversation. "Okay Marcus and Dupree.

We all know what just went down here. Your boy took the fall for the three of you. I have been in a similar situation. It is time for the two of you to make a decision today this minute. You have a choice either you want to live or stay with crew or in the game you will die--."

He pauses to look between the two of us. "I hope you chose to live. Just remember a young man made a sacrifice for you, do not leave him high and dry. You both owe that man your freedom. Are we clear?"

We both nod in agreement. That same day I was done with the game and being crew. I would go to see Trigger every day of my life because if he did not step up as he did. I would be in a cell alongside him.

I found another job working in the computer systems department. It was best for me to quite working with Carol. I needed a clean start, and I continued my visits with Trigger. The arraignment was complete and a court date was set for his sentencing.

Durango and I came each week to see him and leave money on his books. After talking with my dad, he opens a bank account for Trigger. Durango was serious about quitting the game and he married his girl Juanita.

We talk still and kick it as boys whenever time allows. The months are speeding by and the court date for Trigger was here. My family and I attend his sentencing.

The judge takes in consideration that Trigger does not have a record, and sentences him under the guidelines, but he would still have to do ten years.

It has all come down on each one of us, each of us had people in our lives that tried to keep us on the straight and narrow, but we were rough necks. It meant more to be styling named brand gear, chasing every eligible female, counting how many honey's we could take to our bed.

I figured it out after I watched my boy go down to save his crew, and what I surmised is it takes a real man to refuse temptation of the streets. A quick dollar is not what life is about or being a rough neck in the streets, it amounts to nothing, but grief and misery.

It took me a long time to learn that lesson, but I did learn. My dad is still dating my mother and things are serious.

Toney was taking a stroll with Joann on the lakefront the couple holds hands and kiss as they walk alongside the beach.

Time was running out for Toney, he has a life in California and could not keep putting his return on hold. He stops walking and turns to face Joann. It was obvious he has love for her there was no denying that, when he glances at her his heart fills with desire. "Jo, you know you mean the world to me these past months have been trying and nerve wrecking, but the happiest of my fourteen years without you.

He rubs a nervous hand across his neck. "Baby what I am trying to say is I love you Jo, and I don't want to spend another day without you beside me."

Joann was staring in his eyes with love and longing, she clears her throat before she answers. "Toney I don't want to live my life without you either. What are we going to do about it?

She has a tempting smile on her face. He draws her against him kissing her with passion, lust, longing, and love. After he comes up for air, he replies.

"Let's tell our children we are going to remarry and set the date baby. I have been as patient baby and I want you Jo." She hugs his waist looking into his face. "I cannot wait honey. With you is where I belong, even our children know it." They continue walking along the beachfront talking and laughing as one.

Marcus is still committed to Gina their engagement has been a couple of months now, and life was good. He was making great money with his degree and Gina contributes to their future with her income.

The couple was making plans for a wedding in September. Marcus and Gina were sitting at the kitchen table going over their plans, and the doorbell rings. Marcus goes to answer the door.

His mom, dad and sister come inside the apartment. Marcus is surprised to see his family today and wonders what is going on. Gina greets his relatives and offer refreshments.

The family gathers in his living room and Toney begins the conversation. "Son, Gina we came by to let you know that your mother and I are getting married next month and we want our children to be a part of the ceremony." Gina offers her good wishes to both Joann and Toney.

Marcus hugs his dad. He was expecting this news eventually. It was obvious that his parent has never stopped loving each other, and it fills him with joy. Toney continues the conversation.

"Son there is something else, you know my company is in California and since we are getting married. Your mother has decided to transfer her job to California.

What are your feelings on the matter son?" Marcus goes over to his mother she was so happy. He hugs her and stares directly into her eyes. "Mom all I want is for you to be happy.

You have done an excellent job raising Yvonne and me. Mom it is time for you to think of yourself. You have my blessing." Joann leans her head against Marcus shoulder. "Son that means the world to me that both of you love me enough to let me be happy."

Yvonne joins the group she was crying with joy, watching our parents who found each other this was the best day of her life. Things were looking up for the Harris family. The day's go by without incident, Marcus continues his work and enjoying life with Gina.

Toney and Joann move forward in their relationship, both nervous about their pending nuptials. Trigger is doing his time officer Ortega stops by occasionally to visit. His life has taken a backward spiral down, and he ponders how everything went so wrong.

The only comfort is his boys true to their word both come to see him in this hellhole. Most times, he is on lock down fighting with other inmates to protect his manhood.

You could not trust men that have served long stints of time. Danger waits around each corner, and he prays each day that he has the strength to survive in the joint. He tries to find positive in the negative, attending classes and taking courses, but one particular day Trigger was on his way to the laundry area, and crosses paths with an inmate that has beef.

He was trying to avoid as much trouble as possible, but it was not to be. The inmate was beat down in front of his crew by Trigger and that was not acceptable. The man slides the shank into his pocket, and works alongside Trigger in the laundry room.

Chapter 12

He signals a fellow inmate to clear the area, once the room is clear he attacks. The incident takes Trigger by surprise he fights for his survival. The inmate is swinging the shank at Trigger grazing his face with the weapon. He meets with fist to his upper jaw but the man continues the attack on Trigger.

In the scuffle, the inmate makes contact with his flesh piercing Trigger in his side. Trigger was not going to go out lying down. He summons all his strength to deflect the attack. Another inmate named Blaze comes to Triggers rescue the man has the attacker in a full nelson squeezing the man's neck with force. The inmate submits and drops the shank.

Trigger holds his side applying pressure to stop the bleeding. The man holding the attacker introduces himself as

Blaze. Blaze was six feet one-hundred ninety pounds of solid muscle, and doing a ten-year bit. Blaze inquires, "You alright man?" Trigger nods still holding his side as blood oozes from the wound. Trigger replies. "Good looking out man." Blaze responds. "No problem man my name is Blaze. What is yours? Where are you from man?" "They call me Trigger and I am from the Chi."

The man releases the attacker with a warning. "You had better fall back brother, next time you will be on the receiving end." The inmate scurries out the laundry room, thankful Blaze did not kill him. Blaze has a reputation in the joint he was a member of the Muslims over five thousand strong.

He watches the man running from the area and continues the conversation with Trigger. "Hey man you have better let the nurse take a look at that you're bleeding all over the place." Trigger looks at his hands covered in blood he nods his agreement and once again thanks the man. "Look brother I appreciate your assistance man."

Blaze face breaks into a smile. "Cool man you may want to chill with me and my crew. You have to pick your associates in this place with care." Trigger thinks on it and replies. "Cool man maybe I will run into you later. Thanks brother."

The wound takes eighteen stiches and Trigger stays on high alert after the incident. He was learning fast in the joint and his association with Blaze was to his benefit. Blaze was a good brother, and he shares with Trigger as him he got caught up in the game. He mentions his brothers were all gang bangers and he followed their footsteps. In the end, he catches a case for strong-armed robbery of a bank.

He mentions leaving behind a two-year-old daughter and his girl of fifteen years. The man takes a hard look at Trigger and replies. "Man the reason I am telling you this young brother is to help you cope while doing your time man.

Learn from this man and never come back here for nothing. I have done time twice now this is my last stay man that is real talk." Trigger appreciates Blaze friendship and takes his advice. Today is visiting day for Trigger and his boys are on schedule.

He appreciates their loyalty, but accepts the reality that eventually the visits will cease overtime and he dreads the thought. Durango was mentioning his marriage to his girl. "Yeah man I am enjoying married life brothers.

It keeps a brother out the streets. We all know Juanita is not having it." Trigger smiles at the comment, and replies. "How is my mom's man? Have you checked on her for me? She does not come to visit, and most of her letters make no sense. I take it she is to buzz to realize what she is writing."

Marco could see the concern on his boys face and the hurt. It would mean a lot to Trigger if he knew his mother was good, and he does not have the heart to tell him she is still getting high at every opportunity. He tries to reply in a cheerful tone. "Yeah man your mom's is good seen her the other day she sends her love man."

A look of relief settles on Trigger. His mother was all he has to depend on, and with him being in the joint. There was no one around to monitor how much smack she is using. The thought of her dying of an overdose was a constant fear for him.

He drags his mind away from those thoughts and asks his boys about the goings on in the streets. "What's good? Marco when you going to make Gina a wife? How's your parents man?" Marco answers his questions before time runs out and the visit comes to end.

Durango and Marcus leave the prison together and converse along the way home. Marcus starts the conversation, "look here Durango man let's check in on Trigger's mom. I hate lying to him man it would mean a lot to him if we know for sure she is good."

Durango replies, "Cool man I could tell she is resting heavy on his mind dog." The men turn off the expressway and start in Triggers mother's direction. As soon as they pull up to Cynthia's house, it was apparent that a crack party was going on.

Marcus and Durango are not prepared for what awaits them, but they continue up the stairs and knock on the door.

Dope feins stumble down the stairs while crap games go on at the bottom of the steps. It was another rundown neighborhood. The area makes both men leery. A loud voice cursing greets them at the door. Cynthia's hair matted to her head. The clothes she is wearing are winkled, unclean, making her look dirty.

The woman's appearance proves she has been awake for months and her build is frail from lack of eating and rest. "What in the hell do you motherfuckers want?" She was standing with her fist balled leering at us. I respond to the question.

"Mrs. Davis, hello I am a friend of Triggers, my name is Marcus. We just stopped by to check on you. We went to see your son today and he was concerned about you."

The woman rolls her eyes and cocks her head. "Fuck that! You come to get some ass or not? I will do you both for forty dollars." She was pulling at her dirty clothing trying to tempt us. Durango and I mouths both drop open neither of us expecting the reply.

"I don't have all fucking day you are interrupting my business. You want me to fuck you or suck you. What's it going to be?" We both reply at once, "Neither Mrs. Davis." I try to reason with the woman she is clearly gone on drugs and not thinking straight. "Mrs. Davis is there anything we can do for you? It would really mean a lot to Trigger if you would stop in on him. He is worried about you."

The woman looked at us as if we are intruders. She places her hand on slim hips and replies. "Fuck that! I raised his no good ass. I have served my time with the motherfucker, and do not come over here trying to get up in my business. If you motherfuckers want to help me then give me some dope or money, if you got neither then get the hell gone."

She does not wait for a reply, and wobbles back to the door slamming it in our face. Durango and I are shocked not knowing what to say we look at each other dumbfounded, and roll out of this neighborhood as quick as possible conversing along the way.

Durango replies, "Man dog I can see why Trigger is so wild man look how he was brought up." I think on the information and respond, "Man what am I going to tell Trigger now man? You see for yourself that she is a hype man. How do I break that shit to our boy?"

Durango rubs his hand across his brow. "Look Marco man we will have to tell him the truth man at least we tried dog." I agree and we continue to our destination. I drop Durango off and head for home Gina was waiting on me. "Hi boo. How was your day today?"

She has a sexy outfit on and looks dam good. I stroll into the room drawing her close and put some sexual healing on her ass. We did not make it to the bedroom I was too busy getting her out of her clothes pulling off her panties with my teeth.

Once I complete that task. I roll that wide ass over slapping it down knees forward against the coffee table as I slide in behind her. She braces herself with her hands on the table and I plunge into her like a mac truck taking her by storm.

I released, my frustration and worry in quick hard thrust. She loved it mumbling some incoherent words and begging me to continue my thrust. My hands are full of breast tugging on them as I lean over her climaxing in unison both of us breathing erratically.

We could not move for the longest time still sensitive from the lovemaking. We collapse on the floor holding on to each other not wanting to let go. She turns to me and replies. "Marcus I love you."

Toney and Joann's wedding takes center stage, it was time for their nuptials and the church was crowded. Stacy, Travis, and Durango stand in as grooms. I was the best man for my dad while Gina, and a couple of my mom's coworkers stand in as bridesmaids and Yvonne was maid of honor.

My chest swells with pride watching my parent's take it to the next level. Man this was one of the happiest day of my life. After the ceremony, we raise our glasses with a toast to my parent's wishing them both a happy life together. My dad eyes are shining with admiration and so was my mom.

Durango and I approach the circle containing my dad's friends Travis and Stacy. I drop a brother man handshake on them both and proceed with conversation. "What up Stacy? You look sharp man." Stacy flashes his gold tooth styling a tailored suit with matching hat.

You could tell my pops friends were all old school players. Stacy replies, "What up Marco man? I hear you are doing great things man working and maintaining out here." I acknowledge the statement. "Yeah man doing my own thing out here, but staying on the straight and narrow."

He shakes his head with approval. "That is what I like to hear young brother. I told you a long time ago you have to potential to be in the game man. I shake Stacy's hand then Travis before I turn to speak with my pops. "Congratulation dad, today was a good day, mom is glowing with happiness. I have never seen her so elated."

My dad leans over and whispers in my ear. "I plan on that smile staying on your mother's face son. You know she is not alone, this was long overdue." I hug my dad and my mother makes her way over interrupting our conversation. "Well seeing the two most important men in my life showing love makes my day."

She leans in and kisses my dad on the cheek. He places a protective hand around her waist, winks at me then guides her off for a dance. Durango makes his way over we talk for a while before Yvonne, Dale and Gina make their way over. Durango leaves the group after his wife Juanita comes over and asks for a dance.

We do our handshake and he exits the group. My sister is still laughing and crying each time she looks at our mother and father are showing love and affection. She takes a minute then asks me with seriousness. "Okay Marcus mama and daddy have taken the step. When can we expect you and Gina to take the plunge?"

I look down at my sister trying to play matchmaker and reply, "We are going to tie the knot in a couple of months." A smile creeps over her face, "Good I will help Gina with the arrangements.

I am happy for you Marcus, never thought my brother would change his ways, but glad you have." I hug my little sister and note the pride in her voice. The evening continues with laughter and my parent's take their leave from the party to be alone.

I finish the night out with my boy Durango and Gina we sit and talk for a few more hours before the night ends. Gina was offering both of our services with clean up and once we complete the task we head for home. A couple of weeks pass since the wedding and life continues at a fast pace.

Gina and I still working on our relationship and I still find time to check in on my boy Trigger this particular visit was strange at the least. Durango and I wait in silence for Trigger to come and have a visit when he reaches us he looks serious at us both.

"Look man have you heard anything from my mom's? I have tried several times to reach her and the phone is disconnected man. I am worried about her being on her own man." I take the lead, "Trigger man we went a couple of weeks ago to check in on your momma—." He pauses. "Man it does not look good, she is still getting high dog, and would not listen to reason."

Trigger slumps in his chair with a look of frustration. He replies, "Thanks dog I appreciate you two trying to look out for her man. I need a couple of favors from you both." We sit straight in our chairs waiting for Trigger to continue.

He searches for the right words, and gives us a penetrating stare. "Look man check on my mom's again dog let me know how she is that would make me rest easier knowing she is cool.

The next favor I need is—." He pauses again, "Man look I know you two are putting your life on hold running up here to see me dog. Brothers please stop coming back here man. There is no point, I am here for a grip man and seeing you two makes it harder for me to cope with what goes down in this place."

Durango answers first, "Trigger man we have been down with each other for a lifetime man we can't turn our back to you man." I answer, "Trigger dog you made the ultimate sacrifice we are crew, and boys since we were knee-high. That is something that will never change dog."

Trigger hears the sincerity in both men, but it would be a selfish act on his part to ask them to continue checking in on him for the next ten years. He made his decision before they came to see him and would see it through. "Look brothers I am in here fighting every day to protect my manhood in here. I have made a couple alliances to help make some of these punks easy up, but I have to stay up on my game.

The last incident almost cost my life. Sometimes I think that would be the best alternative. You never want to experience life behind bars man. Do this for me brothers stop coming up here to see me, if I make it outa here alive. I look forward to kicking it with my boys."

Trigger left no room for argument from his boys. It was time to face facts the possibility of him leaving the joint alive was slim. Gang violence was raging in the prison and several brothers have beef with Trigger. He accepts the inevitable he would die inside these walls.

We kept our word with Trigger and went back a couple weeks later to check on his moms. The sad thing about the visit is she was murdered by one of her dope Fein boyfriends, and left dead for weeks in her home. We made another trip to the prison to see Trigger and give him the bad news.

This time I was worried about his mental state the pressure of being locked up and now the loss of his mother was almost too much for him to bear. He was adamant about our visits and this was the last time I came back to see him.

I continued to write some times he would reply others not. My wedding to Gina happen a couple months later we got married in a church. Gina's mother and dad was there my parent's, Yvonne, Dale, Durango, and Juanita attend.

Stacy and Travis came, and it was a beautiful day. When I glance over at my bride, it leaves no doubt Gina was the woman for me. Once we unite as man and wife we celebrated the occasion at one of Chicago's finest hotels.

The DJ played the right sounds, drinks were overflowing and everyone had a good time. Gina and I decided to go to California with my parent's for our honeymoon.

Life in California was different from life in Chicago, and it seems to blend well with my mother. She was happy and giddy true to my pops word a smile stayed on her face. My dad took us all out for dinner and the family vibe is what is hot these days.

Meanwhile back in Chicago my boy Durango is living the life of a happily married man when his life takes a turn. The witness named Troy Gibson was release from police protection after Trigger admits to the double homicide.

What no one knew is Troy was a cousin of Corey and his homeboy, even though he was at the scene when Marco's crew tried to eliminate them. He survived Marcus accidental gunshot. The man sits back at the bar planning every move.

He has one of Marcus's crew in lock down. Troy was intent on seeing street justice served. He would be the executioner…. Troy lays in wait talking with snitches of the hood gathering information on Durango and his where bouts. So far, he knows where Dupree (Durango) works lives and hangs out. He also knows that he is married and his wife works for public works.

One particular afternoon Dupree was leaving work, and stops in a local bar before heading home. He has a couple of beers unwinding from a day on the job. He checks the time on his watch. It was time to strike out he promised his wife Juanita they would go to see a movie. She has been bugging him about it for a week.

As he pulls on the leather quarter length, coat and adjust his hat ready to leave the establishment. A man stops him making idle conversation. "What's up brother looks like you bout to bounce." Dupree never thinks twice about the man or his comment, and gives a dry reply, before he continues out the door.

Troy watches Dupree go out the door and follows. The parking lot is empty people inside having a good time. Troy waits for Dupree to unlock his car door and pounces. The incident takes Dupree by surprise and sharp pain floods his body.

He staggers against a vehicle holding his neck. His hands are wet with blood, and he turns to face his attacker with a questioning stare. The man answers the question with malice. "It came back to bite you. You do not even remember me. I was the witness you left behind when you and your crew attacked my cousin Corey and left us for dead. How does it feel motherfucker to know you're going to die?"

Dupree eyes go wide with the memory. His mind replaying the murders and his body weakens from loss of blood. Another sharp pain rips through him as the man plunges the knife into his stomach gashing it wide open.

Dupree died in the parking lot on his way home. Troy walks away without a backward glance into the night, with a feeling of euphoria. Justice was about to go down for his family, and he would not quit until Marcus entire crew is gone.

Chapter 13

I was still enjoying my new marriage to Gina and spending time with my parent's everything was good until I received a frantic call from Juanita. She was hysterical barley able to speak. In a rush she tells me, Durango was dead.

My heart stopped beating with the news, my mind refusing to believe what she was saying. It could not be possible not my homeboy. I slow my breathing and steer my mind back on the conversation. "Juanita, how did he die?"

I was screaming into the phone trying to get answers. She calms down long enough to complete a sentence. "Marcus she sobs, I don't know who did this. Dupree was at a local bar after work waiting on me. We were supposed to go to a movie and dinner.

Another sob, someone found him lying in the parking lot next to his car. He was on his way home and somebody

murdered him." There was another racking
sob. I swallow hard my throat constricts
with pain and disbelief. I try to calm Juanita
down.

"Look Juanita calm down, Gina and
I are catching a flight back this afternoon. I
got you ma." She answers in a deep breath
filled with relief. "Thank you Marcus, I
cannot believe Dupree is gone." Racking
sobs overtake her and the call ends.

I slide down to the floor holding my
phone against my head and this time tears
fall. This was my homeboy gone, and we
just kicked it a couple of months ago. Now
he was gone never coming back.

Gina sits on the floor next to me
holding me in her arms trying to comfort
me. She takes one look at my face see the
tears I always refused to unleash and she
holds me in her arms. The sounds coming
from the room where the sound of a
wounded animal as racking sobs overtake
me.

Once the tears subside, I whisper in
a hoarse voice after a couple of minutes,

"Dupree is dead Gina they found him in a parking lot stabbed to death." She bows her head against mine and we cried together. I talk with my dad explaining about Dupree, and he offers to return with Gina and me.

I refused help; it was time for me to be a man my dad could not save me all the time. My parent's take us to the airport we are on our way home. A few days later Stacy was checking one of his girls in the street about her earnings being a little light.

A couple of brothers from around the way approach him. Stacy recognizes Bass the other man was neighborhood hype. The man named Bass lights a cigar and mentions what is up in the streets. "What up Stacy, you heard about that fool they found in the parking lot a few days back?"

Stacy was always interested in the goings on in the city. He leans against the Cadillac and listens, "What fool would that be man?" The man looks at Stacy as if he was slipping on his game, and not up on street business. "I heard he was a college boy man, the brother just got married a short time ago. I believe he used to hang out with a couple of his partners and you man."

Stacy straightens up from a lean, curiosity picking his interest. "What's the brothers name man." Bass is always trying to make a dollar, and continues with his story. "Well brother that is going to cost you.

My pockets are light man. What's it worth to you?" Stacy's mind is moving fast pace, the only college boys that have kicked with him are Marcus and his crew. He was beginning to panic was it Marcus body they found in the parking lot?

Stacy snatched the man by the collar shaking him until his teeth rattle. "Don't play with me Bass, who was it?" Bass is nervous, but needs a couple dollars to get another hit. "Tell you what Stacy let me hold ten dollars and I will tell you everything you want to know." Stacy thinks on the proposition, reaches in his pocket and pulls out a ten-dollar bill.

"Spill it Bass I am not in the mood for bullshit." The man swallows nervously and continues the story. "Word on the street is the brother's name was Durango man. Talk around town is he was murdered by a cousin of a dude named Corey, from what I got of it there was beef and this dude Durango was crew with Trigger and Marco."

Stacy was listening if what Bass say's is true then Marco was in danger. He curses under his breath. "Damn, look here Bass I will give you a twenty if you keep me up on that particular information." The man holds out his hand for the extra money and walks away from Stacy.

There is no need to involve Toney with this news. He and Joann just got married. They definably did not need any more bad news. Stacy decides to make it his business to look out for Marco. He yells at his girls to come over to the car. He gives strict orders to keep their ears open for any strange johns bragging about a recent murder, and report back to him.

He turns and walks into the building to buy a drink. With a drink in hand, he places a call to Marco. The phone rings a couple of seconds and Marco answers. "What's up Stacy --?" There was a short pause, "Hey Marco man, I am sorry about your boy Durango man. I got word a little while ago. Marco look here young brother we need to talk, can you meet me on thirty-first at the neighborhood bar? It's is real talk young blood."

I pause for one second before I reply, "yeah I can meet you Stacy and thanks for the condolences. Give me twenty, and I will be there." The call ends and Marcus tells Gina about the meeting while going out the door. He makes it to the bar and Stacy was by a booth standing to get his attention.

Once I come over and do a handshake Stacy cuts to the chase. "I'm glad you could make it, and here's the deal Marco. I had a conversation this morning with a local hype named Bass.

The brother mentioned Durango's murder, and word on the street is Corey's cousin survived the shootout with your crew. The cousin is on a vendetta --." He waits a second and continues. "From what I gather the cousin is the same dude who sent Trigger to prison. You feel me?" My breath stops. This could not be happening; my mind goes over that day.

Trigger and Durango killed two of these brothers. The cousin survived my bullet when the gun accidentally fired. Realization came down hard, and I look at Stacy and reply, "I know who this cat is, my gun fired on accident. We were in a scuffle with these cats man.

Now Trigger is doing a ten year bit and Durango is dead that leaves me man." Stacy leans back in his seat, "Checkmate, I think you see the severity of the situation. That is why I am pulling your coat young brother, are you strapped or do you need my nine?"

I swallow hard thinking that this is what it comes down to kill or die in these streets. Stacy is waiting on my reply. I answer the question. "I am good Stacy you don't have to worry man. I got this." "If you need me Marco hit me up, I got you."

A look of concern was on Stacy's face not convinced by my statement, but willing to let the conversation end. We have a couple more drinks and I make an exit. When I leave the bar the rain was coming down, and the city noise muffled. I walk to my vehicle apprehensive of every sound not knowing what to expect.

The ride home gives me time to reflect, and what crosses my mind is how to protect my wife and myself. My mind replays all my deeds from the women to my boys and now murders. Guilt surrounds me in the darkness if I could take back half of the shit I have done maybe I could find the forgiveness that I seek.

A deep breath escapes me it was no use; I chose this path, made my bed hard. I have to turn over in it. I sit in my ride in front of my building a couple more minutes thinking about Durango the funeral is for tomorrow.

My mind drifts to my boy Trigger wondering how he was doing in the joint. He writes me sometimes not as often as he used to, and I miss him. I sit in silence taking a hard look at my life and the choices I have made, and when I weight it out there are many regrets.

I shake the depression and stress that tries to smother me and walk to the front door of my building. Gina was waiting up for me. She greets me at the door, "hey baby, you hungry?" I look at my wife wishing I could share what is on my mind, but knowing it will only make her upset.

Instead, I hold her in my arms and answer her question, "no ma I am good I ate at the bar." The day of the funeral arrived, and I sit waiting for my wife to finish dressing.

She enters the room looking remorseful, I hug her and we walk out the door. We swing by Dupree's and pick up his wife Juanita. Gina and I have made several visits with her since we returned from California.

We try to help when we can. Juanita thanks us both for the support. She has a weak smile on her face not ready to face the task of laying her husband to rest, hell none of us was prepared to let my boy go.

We enter the church where the funeral scheduled to take place. We sit together as the reverend reads the eulogy. My whole being is lost right now; I never thought I would be attending a funeral for none of my boys.

Dupree was always the one who kept it together even when Trigger and I were at each other's throats. My mind goes over the past when we were little boys going to elementary sharing with each other fighting for one another when older boys start problems with us.

My mind remembers the laughter and the hard times we shared. I fast forward to our teenage years together, going to junior high dances. I remember how each one of us tried to impress the same girl. I go over our days in high school when we played basketball, football, and track. The time we attend our high school graduation together and prom.

My fondest memory is when we learned about running game on females, bragging when we scored with a female. Thinking about our times back in the day, I remember lock them away in memory. We view Dupree's body and return to the cemetery.

People gather around the coffin as the reverend reads the last rites. I lend support to Juanita, she is crying and about to collapse reality setting in that this would be the last time she would see Dupree. A tear slides down my cheek my boy is dead and not coming back.

A couple of months later time continues to move forward. I try to go forward with life keeping in touch with my pops and mom. I was on guard watching my back since news of Corey's cousin being on the loose seeking retribution. I go as far as escorting my wife to work and back home to ensure her safety.

My days are going to work with my nine in the glove box or after work; I am strapped waiting for this fool to make a move. I made a promise that I was not taking any more losses. Now nothing has jumped off, I lay in wait for the unknown.

Trigger is still hanging with the Muslims and Blaze, but war is at a boiling point in the joint.

He sits in his cell rereading the letter from Marcus about Durango's murder, and tears fall in silence. The joint was wearing him down battling each day for survival. Life in the joint was nothing like in the streets. He lives his life on the edge never knowing when an inmate with beef may strike.

Blaze does his part and tries to look out for Trigger, but he could not keep him out of harm's way all the time. Inmates feared Blaze and his crew, but even with all his pull in the joint there was always a brother waiting to cross the line. Trigger was counting his blessings each day working out in the yard with other inmates, never expecting something to go wrong.

He was lifting weights with another inmate named Dane, he is confident the man is cool. Trigger has worked out with this brother a few times building trust, today was no different. Dane offers to spot Trigger with the weights, and casually mentions that he needs to increase the weight to build strength.

Trigger lets his guard down in the yard. He trust the other man and was trying to showboat by increasing the dumbbells on the bar adding extra weight. Dane waits for Trigger to settle on the bench laying back prepared to grasp the bar. A gleam enters the man's eyes smirking as Trigger tries to lift the excessive weight.

Trigger gets an unexpected surprise as the other inmate stands closer, and before Trigger realizes Dane's intent it was too late. The man grabs the bar, and forces the weights down crushing his chest. Trigger struggles to get the weight off, but the man is using all of his might and the weight of the dumbbell has to pin him against the bench.

His struggles are in vain and he curses himself for the foolish mistake. The bar weight along with Dane's body mass crushes the chest cavity allowing ribs to puncture Trigger's heart. He stops struggling as the life drains from his body, Trigger died looking at his killer.

The assault takes place in front of inmates on the yard, but none would come forward. No one wants to be the next victim. The inmate checks to see if Trigger is dead then walks away leaving his lifeless crushed body on the bench. When word reaches, Blaze he devastated.

Blaze wanted to save Trigger by guiding him in the right direction. If he saved one brother from this place maybe, it would be penance for his transgressions. The prison notified Marcus of Triggers death he sinks in a chair after reading the letter.

Every one of his crew dead and he was what is left behind. He covers his face in his hands no able to cry after witnessing so much death. He was numb and his heart was hardened. Marcus paid for the burial of Trigger he was not going to let his boy go out in a state funeral.

Once again, he watches as one of his friends laid to rest wondering if he would suffer the same fate. A couple of months later Yvonne and Dale stop by he enjoys spending time with his sister and her husband. Yvonne convinces Marcus to go out with them to relieve some stress.

She also knows Marcus was taking it hard losing his friends. The couples arrive downtown Chicago have some dinner watch a couple bands perform at a nightclub. Gina was enjoying herself and Marcus allows himself to relax and have a good time.

Dale mentions to Marcus about joining a racket club, and he agrees. The men meet up the next day and play racket ball. Dale was bragging about his skills. "Looks like I am going to beat that ass Marcus.

The remark was a challenge and he accepts. In the end, Dale was trying to retrieve the ball and crashes into the wall blackening his eye. Marcus calls after him, "looks like I am the victor man. What you need is a stretcher."

They finish the game in good sprites the day went well. It has been a few months since Durango's death and Troy Gibson is on the move lying low after the murder. He was on a bench reading the paper and runs across the obituaries.

He catches sight of Tyrone Davis (Trigger). A smile touches his lips somebody saved him the trouble. That leaves Marco and he would take care of his ass in a few once the heat dies down.

The man smiles when the time comes he would personally take Marco out and make his death as painful as possible. He balls the paper up with vengeance, what he needs is a whore and a little coke would not hurt either. The man jumps in his ride head over on seventy- first there was always hookers available.

He sits in his car checking out the inventory. A couple of females appeal to him and he calls one of the girls over to the car. Clair walks over to the Johns car; she was a medium build girl not up on street life. She found herself working the street after leaving South Carolina.

She tried to look for legitimate work but did not possess the skills to obtain regular employment. The street life was the only option and she took to it vigorously. A girl has to eat, and closed legs do not pay the bills.

It has not even been a month ago since she escaped a ruthless pimp. He last pimp beat her ass down. She met a couple of girls on the street that bring her in the stables with Stacy's protection. Stacy was fair and treated her with some small amount of respect.

So far, Stacy was the only pimp that did not take to beating his girls, and would split the earnings with her. She could survive with his protection. Clair completes training on the street with the help of Stacy's girls and knows the signs to look for from a John.

If the dude is acting crazy, run for cover. Troy waits for the woman to approach the vehicle. He would not have any trouble enticing Clair in his ride. He has the game down with women and his appearance is not handsome but average looking. The woman leans into his window. "What's up daddy? You are looking for a good time tonight?"

Troy checks her outfit she was thick just the way he likes them. "Yeah baby jump in and let's handle some business." Clair takes a good look at the man. He looks straight, but she makes it clear how much services cost.

"Sure baby, but it will cost you fifty. I do whatever you like." Troy smiles at the woman and opens the door. "Cool, I got your fifty, hop in baby." Clair struts to the other side of the vehicle lifts the handle and slides in. "Where you want to do this at? There is an alley right over there baby?"

Troy responds, "Don't sweat it baby I want to get a room." She sits back against the cushion and ride to a cheap hotel with the man. Once inside Clair ask for payment first. Troy tosses her a hundred dollar bill, and pours them a drink.

The woman accepts the money not believing she has stumbled up on a brother with cash. Troy turns on the radio and asks

the woman to take her clothes off slowly.
He wants to watch her strip. He places a
couple of lines of coke on the nightstand,
and uses a pen to snort a couple of lines.

After he comes up for air, he offers
Clair a line of coke. She accepts with the
drink in her hand, and muses, he wants to
party with me, and he is a good tipper. Troy
is high and the drink intensifies the drugs.
The drugs and alcohol loosens his tongue, he
begins to brag to Clair about handling some
business. She becomes suspicious and
probes further about what type of business.
Troy continues the conversation.

"You know baby take out a cat, I
already killed a motherfucker for taking
advantage of my peeps." Clair is
apprehensive she delves further. "Why did
you take this brother out? Did he harm your
family?" Troy was snorting more coke and
drinking more liquor.

Chapter 14

"Yeah baby I killed a motherfucker in a parking lot a few months back, and I am waiting on the last of his crew, once I put his ass to sleep, I am ghost." Clair remembers Stacy's girls warning her to stay on the lookout for any strange John bragging about a murder in a parking lot and she is scared.

She tries to remain calm hoping all he wants is sex. Troy's eyes are bulged and have a wild look on his face. He was turning aggressive and orders her to masturbate. He sits back on the bed playing with his genitals, and orders her to dance.

Clair knows she is in trouble, but does what the man ask. In the end, Troy rapes the hooker taking her in every position imaginable. Once he satisfies his lust. He retrieves the hundred after dousing her with alcohol and striking a match.

Clair was screaming rolling around on the floor trying to put the fire out. He walks out the door, leaving Clair for dead and burning. He laughs at the mayhem left behind and muses. *The funky bitch thought I was going to pay for some ass.*

Someone hears Clair's screams and call the cops. She wakes in the burn unit with third degree burns. Her face and body burned beyond recognition, and barley hanging on to life. Two weeks later Clair manages to make a call to Stacy, and he comes to the hospital to check on his girl.

When Stacy arrives at the hospital, and enters Clair's room the sight before him was ghastly. Clair covered in bandages from head to toe. He could see some exposed areas with seared flesh. There was no way Clair would be able to make a living on the streets after this; she would never be the same.

Stacy takes a seat next to her bed and places a comforting hand on her seared arm. His mind questions, what sick bastard would harm a woman in this way? "Clair I am here who did this to you?" Clair turns one uncovered eye in Stacy's direction as a tear slides down. She attempts to speak in a weak voice filled with pain. "I have never seen this dude before. He looked straight normal even.

He gave me a yard to go to the hotel with him. Everything was straight until he started doing some coke then he went crazy bragging about wasting some dude in a parking lot a few months back. The last statement grabs his attention.

"Do you remember what this cat looks like?" she replies, "I would never forget that bastard." She goes into detail describing Troy. "He was about five eleven stocky build light complexion and he was driving a black Toyota when I met him." Stacy sits with Clair for about an hour then leaves the hospital

He makes his way to his Cadillac and places a call to Marcus. The phone rings a couple of times before Marcus picks up. "What's up Stacy? What you doing calling me at work man?" Stacy was agitated, passes on the greeting, and cuts to the chase.

"Marco man I need to see you when you get off work young brother. One of my girls is in the hospital. I believe the dude that put her there is the same motherfucker that killed your boy Durango."

Marcus absorbs the information pauses then replies. "I' am sorry about your girl Stacy. Look man I get off at six where you want to meet?" "I will be at the neighborhood bar on fifty first, see you in a few." The men end the call and Marcus sits back in his chair not believing this dude is still causing problems. The one ace in the hole for Marcus is he can identify this dude.

One way or another when Troy comes at him he had better come hard because Marcus was not playing games. Time passes Marcus straightens his suit jacket and pulls on the leather coat, adjust his hat and out the door. He leaves the parking garage driving in the direction of the neighborhood bar.

He reaches over to the glove box retrieving his nine. One the adjustment was complete he open the door and walk inside the bar. Stacy was at one of his favorite booths and Marcus joins him at the table. The men drop a brother man handshake and Stacy starts the conversation.

"Glad you could make it young brother. Here is the deal man as I told you on the phone this dude injured my girl she is laid up in the hospital in serious condition. This cat torched her man.

I think you need to give me the four-one-one on this dude." I was taking a swallow of my drink then put it on the table. "This cat is about five- eleven stocky built and light in complexion, as far as I know man they use to hang out at a neighborhood bar on fifty- Seventh Street.

Maybe we need to make a run over in that direction, and see if I can spot this fool and handle it from there." Stacy was thinking on my words, after a couple seconds he nods in agreement.

"Let's roll Marco. We can take my car, word up man if this fool is in the bar I am going to deal with his bitch ass." I know what Stacy is saying and I reply. "I am with you Stacy. I am tired of looking over my shoulder man."

We exit the bar together and roll in the direction of fifty-Seventh Street. My mind was going over all my losses both my homeboys are dead and this dude Troy was responsible for one of their deaths. I realized when I got in that car with Stacy that I was risking a lot, but payback was egging me on.

I admit that there would be no rest for me until I saw Durango's killer lying in a box. The ride is in silence. Stacy was handling other demons. He did not like the idea of taking Marcus along with him.

He has always tried to steer Marco in the right direction, but this time was different. He had a score to settle and keep Marco safe, if he could get this fool out the way maybe Marco would have a chance at a good life with a woman who loves him.

The thought crosses his mind, but if I fail, we both can end up dead or doing time. Stacy pushes the thought from his mind. He would not fail he was from the streets. We pull up in the parking lot people were standing around conversing. The weather was pleasant still and the streets still damp from an early morning shower.

I was searching the crowd outside when a man catches my eye. "That's him right there." Stacy looks in the direction and sees the man holding his privates talking with a couple of other dudes. We open the door get out and walk in their direction.

Troy looks up recognizes me and takes flight. We are about to run after him when two dudes step in our path, they must be part of his crew. One man puts out his hands to restrain us, and replies. "I don't think so brothers, fall back man.

You aren't about to come up in our spot and start no shit." I tug at Stacy's arm not sure how many of these cats are rolling with Troy. This was not the time or the place. Stacy was from a different generation nothing like mine. He was old school and grew up in a time when brothers scrap for their respect in the streets.

He glances at the man with his hand on his shoulder and the next thing I know

Stacy drives his fist into the man's mouth, knocking the big dude to the ground. His partner was going to try to join the action, but I grab him dragging his ass out the way. Now I am in a fist to cuffs with this dude wearing his ass out like a new pair of shoes. After I was done beating the man down,

I glance in Stacy's direction and he is pistol-whipping the hell out of the other man, I go over pull Stacy by the back of his coat and we dip out. Once we are a safe distance from the scene I reply. "Dam Stacy I never thought you get down like that man." Stacy flashes his gold tooth and laughs at the comment, before he replies.

"Man, I tell you young blood sometimes even a peaceful man has to take a stand. At least we accomplished one thing. I now know what this brother looks like and will be on my peas and ques." I completely agree. I return to the bar retrieve my car and roll out heading for home.

After that day with Stacy, things remain quite no problems since that day. Troy went underground laying low; he monitors his movements in the city. After the altercation with his boys, it was best to wait it out before striking at Marcus. He was not finished taking his revenge not by a long shot.

In time, their path would cross again and once the opportunity presents itself he would make good on the promise to obtain retribution for his peeps. Six months later Clair recovers from the episode, but she's severely damaged no longer able to make a living hooking in the streets.

Stacy knew her career was over and he paid for a ticket for Clair to return home. It was the least he could do for her. He wished he could have settled the score with Troy. No one fucks with his girls and gets away with it, but this was out of his hands.

Time passes without incident I continue working taking care of my wife and visiting with my sister. I regularly check in on my parent's life was good for a long time. Two years later, we celebrate my birthday I made twenty-five still surviving out here and not one word from Troy.

I stay on alert because I know we have unfinished business, and that the incident with Stacy and Troy's crew was not over. I know one-day Troy would seek revenge against me, but was not willing to waste my time worrying about it. What I was not prepared for is how this punk would come at me.

My wife has some news she wants to share. We are having a quite night at home when she approaches the subject. "Marcus, what do you think about having a family baby?" The question catches me by surprise. I stare at my wife in disbelief wondering what exactly she is trying to say. "To tell the truth ma, a family sounds good. What do you have in mind?"

She reaches for my hand puts it to her lips and smile in my direction. "I am pregnant Marcus three months to be exact." I exit my seat go over to my wife drawing her into my arms. I place a kiss on her cheek and reply. "That is the best news in the world Gina.

I am ready to have me a son up in here." She relaxes in my embrace as if she was holding her breath waiting for my response. "Marcus, I was hoping you would be happy with the news.

We are going to need a bigger place." She was smiling up at me. I agree and we start our search. We were moving right along no problems my sister and kids would stop by, Dale and I continued our membership with the racquetball club.

Life was pretty much normal. My parents were coming to town for a visit and the months were rolling on by. Gina and I found a nice townhouse in Hyde Park area lakefront at our front door. None of my homeboys is around anymore and I stop in once and awhile to visit their graves.

My parents arrived and we invite them to stay with us. Mom's is looking good and so was my pops. Their marriage seems to bring out the best in both of them, and that was what I want her to find someone dependable, and my pops fits her to a tee.

Gina is glowing with the pregnancy complaining about her clothes but I can tell she is ready for motherhood. I was putting in overtime to provide for my new family. I spend long hours at my job, but can rest easy that my parents are with my wife.

Stacy calls and dropped by to see my parents, it was all good for the moment. I let my guard down it had been two years since I hear or seen Troy I was about to think he had moved on. I was wrong. Gina was at the end of the pregnancy when she went into labor it was the weekend and I was home.

We leave for the hospital I am excited about my son on his way into the world. I spent every minute with Gina as she went through labor. My family was there elated about being grandparents, and my sister was ready to be an aunt.

Once I see my son. I walk to the window to display him to my family and Gina's. It had been a long delivery, but they came out of it doing fine. A feeling of pride engulfs me I want to teach my son about staying out the game and being a man that stands on his own two feet.

All my hope for the future was about to end the second day of my son's birth. It was raining hard the evening I came to visit my wife and son at the hospital.

I stayed until visiting hours was at an end around nine o'clock at night. It was dark outside winter was on Chicago that instant rain changed over to snow. As I make my way to the parking lot, about to open my door sharp pain vibrates in my head the pain is so severe it takes me to my knees.

My hand clutches at the door forcing myself to get up, another sharp pain. My attacker was hitting me with a baseball bat and I see my assailant. Troy was standing over me ready to swing a deadly blow. Panic sets in on me; this fool was trying to take me away from the people I love the most my wife and child.

My head is bleeding and swelling from the attack. In a few seconds, my whole life flashed before my eyes strengthening my resolve. I was not going to go out like this not like my homeboys, not like a punk. I summon the will to live and fight for my life.

My legs raise and soundly kick Troy in the private, giving me enough time to get to my feet. I was dazed from the blows to my head and bleeding all over the place. The man screams in pain. I tried to kick his balls out of the parking lot.

I turn to my vehicle open my glove box and retrieve my nine. There was not going to be any looking back for my family or me. Troy was back on his feet coming at me with the bat in his hand. I aim my gun at his ass pull back the hammer and let his ass down. I let off two rounds each hitting him in the chest.

This time it was no accident I killed Troy in self-defense. I pick up my cellphone and call the cops, hospital security witness the attack in the parking lot and no charges filed against me. It was over now I could finally breathe without worry of retaliation.

The Hospital security escorts me into emergency. The Doctor takes some x-rays and bandages my wounds. I made a report of the incident with an officer then admitted in the hospital. My parent's arrive at the hospital worried about damage to my brain. A week later, the hospital released me with a clean bill of health.

My wife was at home now with my son. I still suffer major headaches from the incident with Troy, but it was a small price to pay for my family's safety. Four years later our son is walking and talking now. Gina and I moved from Chicago a year after my assault.

I was ready to put distance between Chicago and myself after that. There were too many bad memories for me there. We moved down the street from my parent's in California.

With their help, we were able to buy, a nice three-bedroom house Gina is pregnant again, and I am expecting a daughter on the way. Our life is truly good now. I decided to author this book in hopes that it may give encouragement to our young people.

I hope it does not take you as long as it took me to learn to stay away from the game. Gina was coming to the study as Marcus sits writing his novel "Playing the Game." "Honey put that manuscript down spend the day with me and little Marcus." "My wife needs me and so does my son."

He closes his manuscript and joins his family.

From: Yours truly

Marcus Terrell Harris

The end

ABOUT THE AUTHOR

Dorothy W. Cosey (1962-Present) was born in a small town in Southern Lower Michigan, the mother of five children discovers she likes to write books, her first title was Lily, and she continues to write western and modern day romance novels. Her latest works include title Kendra, The Perfect Lover, and Playing the Game.

Dorothy enjoys spending time with friends and family, she is currently working on a Bachelor's degree in Information Technology. Dorothy is committed to bringing her readers action and adventure in each novel, she strives to make your reading experience one to remember by providing memorable characters and unexpected twist in each work.

www.ingramcontent.com/pod-product-compliance
Lightning Source LLC
Chambersburg PA
CBHW070446030726
47503CB00004B/914